TRADING SALVOS

A Kate Adams Novel

HOLLY A. BELL

ISBN: 0692710787
ISBN 13: 9780692710784
Library of Congress Control Number: 2016907763
Tolling Bell Press, Palmer, AK

To my husband Eldon who tolerates my writing habit and other assorted flaws.

CHAPTER 1

May

Kate pressed her hands against the tiled wall of the shower and bent forward to let the warm water wash over her head and neck. She had been crying, again. She missed him terribly, but the grief had gone on too long.

Her husband, Max, had disappeared in Singapore over four months ago and was found dead nearly two months later near a lake in Ponggol Park. A software engineer by trade, he also worked as an adjunct professor accompanying a group of Master's degree students on an educational tour of Asian financial markets. The local authorities shared little information about the circumstances of his disappearance and cremated the body before releasing it to the FBI agents dispatched to oversee the investigation. His death remained a mystery, but Kate realized it was this lack of closure that she had been using as an excuse to continue the tears. *Today is the day.*

Kate toweled off as she looked in the mirror with a sense that she hadn't seen herself in a long time. She scolded her reflection, "Dr. Adams, you need a haircut and have developed dark circles under your eyes". As she tried to revive her face with moisturizer, she wondered if cucumbers actually helped puffy eyes or if that was an urban myth perpetuated by Hollywood.

Wrapped in a towel, Kate picked up the pile of laundry she had sorted onto the bedroom floor and placed it into a laundry basket. She walked to the wicker hamper in the corner of the room, took out the T-shirt resting at the bottom, and threw it over her shoulder. The walk to the laundry room was slow and careful as the basket perched on her hip was encouraging the towel to slide off. In the laundry room she added detergent and fabric softener to the washing machine and placed the laundry from the basket into it. Tipping her head to the side, Kate rubbed her cheek against the T-shirt resting on her shoulder and smiled weakly. Bringing the shirt to her face, she inhaled deeply. She could still smell him. His deodorant. His perspiration. He had been happy and healthy, but now he was gone. *This is the moment.* She breathed deeply and released the breath with a sigh. Kate removed the towel from her body and threw it, along with Max's T-shirt, into the washer, closed the door, and turned it on. She closed her eyes, said a prayer, and accepted it was the only closure she was going to get.

Kate walked, in the nude, to the kitchen where she fixed a salad to carry to work for lunch. Returning to the bedroom, she lay down on the bed and placed a cucumber over each eye.

Chapter 2

Four Months Earlier

January

"Really mother, I love living here", Dr. Kate Adams said into her car's Bluetooth microphone as she pulled into the parking garage at the Anchorage International Airport. She thumped the back of her head against the seat's headrest a few times to suppress the scream she wanted to give vent to. *I can't believe we're having this conversation again*, Kate thought to herself as she rolled her eyes and exhaled loudly successfully diminishing the urge to shriek.

"But Katie, Margie's boy Frank is practicing medicine at the Mayo clinic and Betty's oldest, Emily, is working at the White House. The White House for goodness sake! I just don't understand it. You had offers from Georgetown and UCLA after graduate school, but you had to have an adventure and run off to take a job at the University of Alaska. You said you'd stay for two years, it's been 10, when are you going to settle in at a proper university?"

"Well, Mom, I met Max and fell in love with him *and* Alaska so I committed to both for life. I can't imagine living anywhere else now. Besides, the Palmer campus is beautiful and I can walk out the door of Snodgrass Hall and go hiking whenever I want."

"I just don't want you sacrificing your career because of a man. Max would move if it helped you professionally, wouldn't he? I mean, I love Max, but he's a software developer, he could do that anywhere. I just refuse to believe you will get the same recognition as a finance professor in Alaska as you would if you were at Harvard or NYU. Your uncle Robert is concerned too; it's all he can talk about when we're together. We just think you have so much talent." There was a whiny, nasal quality to her mother's voice when she nagged that grated on Kate's nerves. Her mother was trying to force herself to sound sweet and concerned, but the image it evoked in Kate was of honey being poured on a barbed wire fence.

"Mother," Kate said firmly, "Max has worked hard to develop MAK software as a reputable firm and I helped him build it. Did you know, in the early days I helped him develop several computerized trading programs for two Wall Street firms? That's kind of a big deal," Kate paused for her mother's response, but there was silence. She continued, "He has 21 employees now who rely on him and dozens of clients from Wall Street to the Alaska oil fields. I can't ask him to walk away from that. Plus, I'm successful here in my own right. Thanks to my research I'm a recognized global expert on financial market structure and risk management and I get to do consulting for cool organizations like the Securities and Exchange Commission and the Department of Homeland Security. I'm having fun and enjoying my work, why isn't that enough?"

"I'm just saying Katie, if you can have that much success in Alaska, imagine how successful you would be at MIT or Penn State." Kate could picture her mother frowning and shaking her head in disbelief at Kate's disinterest in ruling the world of finance and rewarding her mother with bragging rights.

"Mom, listen, I need to go, I'm flying to DC tonight. I'll talk to you again soon." Kate disconnected the phone before her mother could utter a reason to make her feel guilty about doing so.

After locking the car door and removing her suitcase from the trunk, Kate walked carefully across the icy parking lot to the terminal. Three days earlier Max had left for Singapore and now Kate was at the Alaska Airlines terminal, preparing to take an overnight flight to Reagan National. In two days she had a speaking engagement at a Washington, D.C. think tank luncheon for lobbyists, policy wonks, and journalists on the pros and cons of limiting regulatory intervention in financial markets. While Kate was being brought in to argue the position against additional regulation and taxation, it was a difficult time to hold such a position. While financial markets were performing well in the United States, concerns about income equality had been rising due to a global recession and the numerous challenges it was creating for society.

As Kate approached the terminal door she was confronted with one of the outcomes of the deep recession the U.S. was entrenched in. A family with three young children was standing just outside the door, looking cold and tired in their threadbare Sunday best. The father saw Kate and began looking around anxiously for any airport police in the area. Seeing none, he approached Kate, "Excuse me ma'am, the plane tickets took the last of our cash, do you have any dollars you could spare? I've got a job here in the oil fields and I start tomorrow, I'm just trying to get through the week until I get paid. I need a place for my family to stay and some food. Can you help?"

Kate talked with the family for a while and believing their story to be legitimate, opened her wallet and pulled out a $100 bill she kept there for occasions like these, when someone needed help. It was an all too common occurrence lately.

Helping the family didn't leave Kate feeling joyful, it only increased her anxiety about tomorrow's luncheon. How could she convince a room full of people during times like these that the answer to the country's woes existed in its people and not the government? Especially when so many people couldn't afford to buy bread and milk?

Kate had been told that wine would be served with lunch and she was glad. Hopefully it would serve to quell her own anxiety and soften the sharp edges of her audience. She tried to push thoughts of tomorrow out of her mind.

Taking a seat at the gate, Kate noticed a group of young service members sitting across from her chatting enthusiastically.

"I'm so excited," said one of the two women in the group of six, "I really hope I make it through the school."

"It'll be fine," said the redheaded male sitting next to her. "You're smart, you did great in basic training and you've been flying general aviation airplanes since you were fourteen. Learning to fly a drone should be a snap for you, I'm not worried."

"And," added the other woman in the group, "if we're flying drones we get to work stateside and won't have to deploy to a war zone. That's a significant incentive for me to work hard and not fail."

Paradoxically, on the television directly above their heads the war in the Middle East they were hoping to keep a safe distance from was raging as CNN was broadcasting live coverage of artillery fire in Turkey. The announcer in Atlanta was discussing the timeline of events that led to the U.S. and its allies joining what now appeared to be an emerging World War designed to push back an expanding effort by radical Islamists to expand a new Muslin State. "The conflict," the anchorwoman said, "has been complicated by Iran announcing diplomatic efforts to rebuild a Persian Empire, prompting Turkey to enter the conflict in the name of recreating a modern-day Ottoman Empire."

A few minutes later, the anchorwoman introduced their Wall Street correspondent Gordon Brewer, who was live in the studio. "Gordon, we've been watching the images coming out of Turkey this evening of what appears to be an escalating conflict in the Middle East. Can you tell us what this means for Wall Street in the coming days?"

"Well, Peggy, U.S. financial markets have performed very well during this conflict so far thanks to significant government spending on the war and an influx of capital from Europe, since their economies remain stressed due to mass migration pouring in from war torn countries. I would expect positive market returns to continue in the short-run. However, the financial sector does have some political problems that may impact longer-term returns. For example, Russia is leading an effort to have the dollar removed as the global currency and three days ago a cyber attack penetrated the New York Stock exchange. Fortunately that attack was quickly identified and neutralized, but if these types of events continue, it could cause problems for markets as investors lose confidence in their security."

Kate's thoughts drifted back to tomorrow's luncheon. She would be the first of three speakers, not an enviable position for a free-market idealist in a time of economic and political crisis. The thought of standing up in front the audience reminded her how frustrated she had become with her career. A brief stab of depression moved through her. Kate knew that by the time the final speaker, a Marxist economist, had extolled the virtues of a government redistributing resources according to each individual's needs and the evils of corporate America, her words warning against over regulation and increased taxation of financial markets would be but a faint memory. Thank goodness for wine.

CHAPTER 3

The morning of Kate's speech was punctuated by heavy, wet snow in the Washington, D.C. area. While the snow had tapered off by the time Kate was ready to leave for her event, deep slush dunes remained in the gutters and slick, icy patches dotted the sidewalks. Kate dropped her shoes in her briefcase and pulled on her heavy snow boots before exiting her hotel and heading for the Tysons Corner Metro station. Though she looked out of place in her arctic boots, Kate appeared to be the only person she passed with warm, dry feet. She allowed herself to feel a momentary sense of superiority; if civilization broke down, she might be among the survivors.

As she descended into the Metro station the warm, musty subterranean air enveloped her. To her right a man was playing a keyboard and singing *"Bridge Over Troubled Water"* with so much tenderness within the chaotic station, Kate was moved to drop a five-dollar bill in his bucket. It was late-morning and most of the commuters were gone and had been replaced by tourists, maps in hand, discussing which museum or shopping center they could sprint through before lunch. A glum-looking girl of about 14 sat slumped on a bench, arms folded, obviously unhappy with her family's choice of activities. The train arrived and Kate found a seat as the train began to travel down the Silver Line. She thought about the song *"Bridge Over Troubled Water"*: *Bridge, water, river, flow, change, time, fast, movement, forward, future...*Her word association was interrupted by her need to change trains. When Kate was a child she had made up a word association game that she used on long car trips. She still slipped into it occasionally when her mind was idle. The goal was to start with a word and in less than five word associations find her way back to the original word. She was usually interrupted, as had been the case today, before she finished.

When Kate exited the train at Metro Center to connect with the red-line, she noticed her feet had become too warm in her boots. Perhaps she would have to reconsider her strategy of footwear as a means of apocalyptic survival. She rode the Red Line to the Gallery Place station where she decided to walk the rest of the way to cool down. She arrived at the event 30 minutes early, despite walking part of the way, and was escorted by security to the Green Room to wait. She removed her boots and put on her heels, reviving a feeling of femininity the boots had suppressed. Kate entertained herself by scrolling through her Twitter feed. Someone had posted a picture of a young, shirtless Clint Eastwood leaning against a payphone. Another person had commented, "This is what a real man looks like". Kate hoped being a "real man" didn't require being propped against a payphone or there was no longer any hope for society.

The remaining two speakers and the moderator all arrived within the next 20 minutes. Kate was polite and engaged in brief small talk, but remained distant, preferring to be alone with her thoughts. She used to like talking to people, especially ones who disagreed with her. They provided mental stimulation and allowed her to practice emotional control in her arguments, she liked to let others be the first to resort to name-calling. When someone called her a moron, Kate took it as a signal of victory. However lately she noticed she had been isolating herself more, allowing her thoughts to carry her off to some distant point. It was as though she were stuck, unable to move or grow in an internal conflict that left her feeling somewhat one-dimensional, obsessive and compelled to move toward something unknown that was gnawing at her. While Kate recognized her new state of mind might not be a good thing, she felt helpless to pull herself out of it.

As the luncheon was beginning, Kate and the others walked from the Green Room and through a back door to the event room. The room was set for lunch with fifteen round tables that seated six people each. The panel was seated on a low stage at the front of the room that contained a lectern with long tables on each side. Hand-held microphones were also set out for each of the four panel members in anticipation of a question and answer segment. A lunch of kale salad with a balsamic dressing, beef tenderloin medallions, a sweet potato mash, and asparagus was served. Kate sipped her Malbec while scanning the assembled crowd.

The audience was predominantly male and the people unfamiliar to her, with a few exceptions. She knew a few journalists in the audience who had interviewed her in the past and expected them to ask politically motivated questions. While they wouldn't say it out loud, they would be thinking '*moron*' to themselves as she answered. A slice of cheesecake that looked like it had been stamped out in a factory was presented with coffee for desert. Kate asked for a second glass of wine instead.

The moderator moved to the lectern, smiled widely and made some promotional comments about the hosting organization before providing brief biographical introductions for each of the speakers. Kate was invited to the lectern as the first speaker.

The audience listened politely as Kate gave her speech within which she encouraged a loosening of regulation and taxation, and encouraged policy makers to allow markets to fix themselves. The stony stares of the assembled implied they were not enthused about her recommendations. After her concluding remarks, Kate sat down to light applause and the company of her wine glass.

The two remaining speakers were greeted with considerably more excitement. Proposals to use taxes to take a significant portion of profits away from people who earned capital gains from the sale of stocks in order to give money to the poor were presented. Arguments that capitalism is evil, causes climate change, and that it has failed to establish itself as a socially optimal economic system were offered. The audience erupted in enthusiastic applause as the two men finished their presentations. Kate's second glass of wine was gone; she nodded for another.

The moderator announced the panel would now take questions from the audience as Kate's cheeks began to flush from the wine. The first gentleman, a reporter from the Associated Press, rose and directed a question to the third speaker, "Dr. Belcher, you mentioned the need to significantly increase taxes on the returns from investments, what do you believe is the socially optimal tax rate for investments?"

"Thank you, that's an important question." Dr. Belcher paused and took a deep breath to ensure his voice inflected a level of pomposity fitting his expert status, "It is my belief that taxes on capital gains should be raised to at least 70%." Several reporters nodded their heads and scribbled furiously in their notebooks.

Cheeks now at full-flush, Kate turned to her fellow panel member, "Based on what? Who is this benevolent individual who has all information past, present, and future who can decide what the proper tax level should be that ensures a socially optimal market outcome? Isn't it the very absence of such an individual that forces us to rely on markets?"

Briefly stunned by the challenge, Dr. Belcher slowly turned his head back toward the reporter, chuckled, and said, "Well, there's the case for oppression of the working class and chaos in the markets". The assembled offered muttered laughter.

"Dr. Adams", the AP reporter asked, "You seem to have a lot of faith in markets. Is there any scenario under which you believe they may not be good for society?"

Kate thought carefully, eyes rolled toward the ceiling. The wine made it difficult to focus precisely on the reporter, so looking toward the crowd, she replied, "Yes. There are at least two scenarios I am concerned about that need to be guarded against. The first is a cyber attack on the market. We recently experienced an infiltration into the New York Stock Exchange and such an event should never be allowed to happen again. A worst-case scenario could involve foreign governments weaponizing computerized trading in these markets to manipulate currency values, inflation, the prices of raw materials, and securities prices around the globe

A second scenario would be that the regulatory and tax environment could become so burdensome, that capital begins to move offshore to countries that do not independently monitor their markets as well as the U. S. does."

The second speaker, Dr. Kalugin laughed and shook his head. "Come on!," he scolded, "There is no way that will ever happen. Capitalists control markets for their own personal gain while governments put the needs of the people first. That's why we need to move more investment profits to our government. It's to secure our markets and remove income inequality. Besides, the biggest risk facing society today is climate change and capitalism is its greatest contributor. You are worrying about the wrong things."

Kate wondered if this man wrote the slogans for those anti-capitalist rallies disguised as climate change marches, during which they engage in capitalism by selling their socialist newspapers for a dollar and t-shirts for ten without even a hint of irony. To Kate the color in the room appeared to be fading to grayscale and the audience tables seemed to move farther away. She hoped it was the onset of a deep depression and not a stroke. With a sigh of exasperation, Kate concentrated on finishing her third glass of wine.

Chapter 4

Mercifully, the event ended and Kate stepped down from the stage, glass in hand, as a few journalists and lobbyists lined up in front of her to get quotes and exchange business cards. A young reporter from a European publication Kate had never heard of asked a few follow-up questions about her comments regarding capital moving to offshore financial markets. He seemed well informed and sincerely interested in her thoughts. It was a refreshing conversation. If Kate wasn't careful her mood might improve and she would have to stop brooding.

As the journalist walked away, Kate looked up and saw a point of color in the otherwise gray room. He approached in a charcoal suit with a burgundy-striped tie, matching pocket square, and a warm smile. While still handsome, flecks of white were prevalent throughout his once reddish-brown hair. At six foot four he was difficult to miss as he pulled himself away from the wall he had been patiently leaning against and made his way toward Kate. Too bad there hadn't been a payphone nearby.

"Bradman Owen Oakley", Kate greeted her old friend with a warm smile and outstretched arms inviting a hug, "It's been too long".

"Uh-oh", Brad said hugging her tightly, "You used my full name, I must be in trouble".

"Not at all, I'm happy you came Boo." She meant it.

Bradman was Brad's mother's birth name and while some people like Larry David seemed to have two first names, Brad carried what appeared to be three last names. The nickname Kate had given him came from both his initials and his career. He was a spy by trade, a 'spook', who had a distinguished career at the CIA, or so she was told. What he specifically did was unknown to her, but he hated when Kate referred to him as a spy. "Spies are the people who work for us," he always said, "We're Case Officers who run spies."

They had met 15 years earlier at a conference when Kate was in graduate school. Actually, it was less a 'meeting' and more a stalking. Brad had noticed her in the hotel lobby as he arrived with five colleagues to check in—or had he first noticed her in the airport? She wasn't sure. In order to determine her name, Brad allowed her to be in front of him in the queue at the hotel desk. Once Kate had checked in, he asked for the room across the hall from her, as if they were old friends or colleagues. Brad then waited for her to leave her room, followed from a safe distance behind, and stuck his hand in the elevator as the door was about to close. He entered apologetically and introduced himself while Kate pretended not to notice what he had done. She had let the illusion of her ignorance persist for 15 years.

Brad was thirteen years Kate's senior, but they became fast friends and were never at a loss for things to talk about or hiking and kayaking adventures to enjoy. He mentored her in history and politics and picked Kate's brain on issues of finance and economics. They had eventually decided to ruin a perfectly good friendship by becoming romantically involved. As a result, they hadn't seen each other in more than 12 years.

"Look at you, I got old and you haven't changed a bit! I hate men," Kate teased.

"Dr. Adams, you're just as pretty as ever. I heard you were in town and after speaking with you a couple of months ago, I couldn't resist the temptation to see you again."

Kate had broken their long silence two and a half months earlier by calling Brad for some advice. She regularly worked with think tanks on policy issues and a gentleman named Harry Clark—who claimed to operate a small intelligence think tank he'd started after finishing his career at the CIA—had contacted Kate about a year and a half earlier. Mr. Clark claimed to be calling not so much to ask for her expertise, but because he wanted to send her books and articles he thought she would find interesting. She agreed and he sent a book he had authored to campus and began e-mailing articles. A couple of months later, he started asking for her opinion on the articles he'd sent, and later started questioning her on subjects like how to bring down the U.S. dollar as the global currency. Mr. Clark had also begun inquiring as to whether she would be willing to write for him at his think tank, something Kate had done, and was still doing, for several other groups.

When Kate tried to do some research on the organization and Harry Clark, there was little information beyond a website available. When she would push him for information he would back off for a couple of months and then begin the entire cycle over again starting by simply sending her articles. Kate had developed a bad feeling about the situation. There were two possibilities Kate could think of, that he was who he said he was and might be priming her for something. If that was the case, Kate preferred a more direct approach and whatever game he was playing was getting on her nerves. Or perhaps he was someone intent on doing the U.S. harm and she wanted no part of it.

She had called Brad to see if he knew Harry Clark—which she figured he wouldn't tell her even if he did—but more importantly for advice about whether she should continue communicating with him. After a lengthy pause, Brad told Kate he had always trusted her instincts and if she had a bad feeling she should trust them too. He hadn't been much help. It would have been best to just trust her instincts in the first place. Paranoia was not something she generally engaged in, so if the hair on the back of her neck was standing on end, it was probably for good reason. She cut off communication with Mr. Clark and, after a couple of E-mails inquiring if he had said something to offend Kate, she hadn't heard from him in at least six months.

Brad offered his arm to Kate. "Would you like to join me for coffee? It looks like you could use some," he said good-naturedly. Kate set her empty wine glass on a nearby table. As she turned to go she noticed how spectacularly clear the crystal glass was against the white tablecloth, just like the fine Czech crystal she had seen in Krakow years before. The light was hitting the cuts in the crystal just right and the glass sparkled, casting light on the ceiling and walls. It was stunning, like a fine diamond. Her world was beginning to look a little brighter again.

They stepped out into the crisp January air, which was refreshing after the crowded conference room. The sun was shining and the pavement was drying, so Kate carried her boots, while clicking down the sidewalk in her heels. She breathed deeply and became aware of a need to diminish the effects of three glasses of wine. She was a bit dizzy and could feel the burning flush of her cheeks in the cold air. As they walked the short distance to a small coffee shop, a squirrel scolded them from a bare cherry tree planted in a space near the sidewalk's edge and the smell of freshly baked bread wafted out of a nearby deli. She made a mental note to visit that deli sometime.

Upon arriving, Brad ordered a latte for himself and an espresso for Kate, even though that wasn't her usual drink. She didn't argue. He was obviously trying to sober her up, but didn't seem judgmental about her overindulgence, just amused.

They perched on barstools at the window counter that looked out toward the cherry tree. The squirrel had abandoned the tree and was now picking nervously through a nearby garbage can, tail twitching. The sun was trying to come out from behind the clouds.

"That was a tough crowd today, your frustration was palpable." Brad said with a grin, "If it's any consolation, I agree with you and would have joined you in the consumption of wine if I didn't have to go back to the office for a few hours this afternoon".

"I don't think I want to talk about it, I'm feeling a bit defeated. Every time I find an issue I strongly believe I need to take a stand on, I always seem to end up at the crossroads of wanting to fight or retreat to a remote part of Alaska and live off the grid in a yurt. Since I already live in Alaska, I'm not far removed from the yurt". Kate took a long pull on the espresso knowing she was as sensitive to caffeine as she was to alcohol. She'd feel more like herself soon. Brad's company helped, she didn't feel as isolated as she had earlier. "How have you been?" Kate asked with genuine interest as she squeezed Brad's forearm.

"I'm well. Happy. Still single. There have been a few women in my life, but none I felt like I wanted to settle down with. The job makes it somewhat difficult to meet women I don't work with and when I do, the job makes it difficult to trust them. But you already know that". He frowned in a way that implied reflection. "I'm glad you've found someone who makes you happy and I'm also pleased you've continued your work on national issues. When I heard you'd moved to Alaska I was concerned you would start writing papers like 'Five Ermine Skins for an Igloo: A Guide to Alaskan Economics', but perhaps you're saving that topic for after you've gotten comfortable in your yurt". They laughed.

"Perhaps", Kate replied with a grin. She was starting to feel better.

"What are your plans for the rest of your trip?" Brad inquired.

"I leave around noon tomorrow. I'm planning to do some clothes shopping this afternoon. Alaska is a great place to buy furs, but a lousy place to buy suits". She grinned, "Of course, it's also considered socially acceptable to come to work in nothing but a fur."

"My kind of place," Brad returned the grin. Kate missed his companionship. Maybe after all this time they could go back to being friends. "Perhaps we could have dinner tonight, if you have time?"

"Sure. What time?"

"I'll pick you up at 6. Where are you staying?"

"The Regal, Tysons Corner."

"May I give you a ride to your hotel? It's on my way?"

"No, thank you. I think the trip back on the Metro will help clear my head"

"Are you sure? I don't like sending you into the Metro by yourself, I'd hate for you to have your purse stolen or worse". He looked serious. *Still overprotective*, Kate thought.

"I'll be fine. I dare anyone to try to take my purse. There's so much caffeine coursing through my body right now, the fatal blow would descend upon them so fast, they'd never see it coming."

"That's my Kate, still self-confident and stubborn. Just be careful."

"I will." They smiled, hugged, kissed each other on the cheek, and went their separate ways.

Chapter 5

A group of uniformed school children were running up the stairs as Kate descended back into the train station for the return ride to her hotel. When she arrived at the Tysons Corner Station, she was surprised to see the same keyboard player. This time he was playing *Unchained Melody* by the Righteous Brothers. She stopped to listen and a pang of sadness washed over her for Max's absence. Fortunately, he'd be home in a week. She missed him.

As she stood with about ten other people enjoying the song and wondering why a talent agent had not discovered this musician during the past four hours, a man of about fifty walked over to her and bowed.

"May I have this dance?" he asked and held out his hand.

"Yes, you may" Kate agreed, charmed, and they danced slowly to the music. Others began to join them. The gentleman really knew how to dance, but more importantly he knew how to lead, which made Kate feel like she knew how to dance. Kate was struck by the surrealism of dancing in a train station with a man who knew how, to a musician who should have a recording contract. No one would ever believe her. She was savoring the moment.

When the music ended, Kate curtsied to her partner, while the assembled group that had grown to about twenty-five, applauded. She turned and headed for the stairs. As she did, the keyboard player pulled back his sleeve, moved his wrist to his mouth and said, "She's on her way to the hotel".

It was 2:00pm when Kate entered her hotel room to drop off her briefcase and boots before heading across the street to Tysons Corner Mall to do some shopping. She put the briefcase down next to the desk and set the boots on top of her closed suitcase, ran a brush through her hair and headed out again.

Her first stop was at Haagen-Dazs to have a small scoop of vanilla ice cream. Between the wine and the coffee, Kate needed something to settle her stomach. Feeling revived, she walked to Brooks Brothers were she bought two suits. At Ann Taylor she found a short, black sheath dress with a wide leather belt trimmed in silver. *The new dress would be great to wear to dinner tonight,* Kate thought.

Kate moved on to Nordstrom where she bought some more clothes and tall, black Cole Haan boots with three inch heals. The boots would keep her legs warm and dry when she was in D.C., without causing her to be mistaken for a tourist from a farm town in the upper Midwest like her current boots did. On a whim, she also bought a pair of black short boots with a back zipper made from Italian leather so soft they were impossible to resist. At around 4:00, Kate returned to the hotel to get ready for dinner.

The sun had been shining into the hotel room during the afternoon, but had since moved low on the horizon and the room felt cool. Kate adjusted the thermostat to a more comfortable temperature. The morning's events had left her exhausted and trying on clothes had made her hair look like she had stuck her finger into a light socket. Static electricity was not a friend to those with fine hair. She was going to need a shower, but first she turned on the television and switched to a 24-hour news channel to catch up on the day's events. War was still raging in the Middle East and the economy was still struggling. Obviously her speech had not changed the world. At 4:45, Kate jumped into the shower.

By 5:00pm there was a knock on the door. Kate was still in her robe with her hair wrapped in a towel. She looked out through the peephole to find Brad standing in the hallway, holding his briefcase. Kate didn't remember giving him her room number. She opened the door.

"Hi, Boo," she said, "You're early, I wasn't expecting you until six. I'm not ready yet."

"That's okay," Brad said brushing a kiss on her cheek while stepping into the room and looking around, "I finished early and didn't have time to go home, so I thought I'd just come over early while you got ready. I'm not trying to rush you; we still don't need to leave until six. Go get ready, I'll watch the news." He waved her toward the bathroom with his left hand, while simultaneously grabbing the remote from beside the television with his right. He started flipping through the channels, stopping at a different 24-hour news station.

Kate grabbed her clothes, hair dryer, flat iron, and makeup bag and returned to the bathroom to finish getting ready, closing the door behind her.

A few moments after the bathroom door was closed, Brad opened his briefcase and removed an electronic devise that looked like a small, hand-held walkie-talkie with a digital display screen. He started sweeping the room with it, lifting picture frames, lamps, the telephone, and the bed skirt. He even swept Kate's suitcase, purse, and briefcase. On five different occasions he stopped to remove small listening devices including one just inside the sliding handle compartment of Kate's suitcase. He put the devise and the bugs he had removed into his briefcase and calmly went back to watching the news.

After thirty minutes, Kate emerged from the bathroom feeling quite feminine in the new dress and tall boots. It was nice to be out of a suit. "Wow! You look wonderful. Smart *and* hot, how did I ever let you get away?" Brad asked. Kate smiled, treating it as a rhetorical question, as she didn't wish to ruin the evening by reminding Brad about his complete inability to commit. Yes, she and Brad were better as friends than they ever would have been as partners. Kate was happy she had waited for Max.

They watched the news together for a while and shortly before six, Brad called down to the valet to have them bring his car around. After a quick check of her lipstick, Kate grabbed her coat and the two of them took the elevator to the lobby where they could see Brad's idling car outside with the driver's side door standing open. The valet opened the hotel door and Brad rushed to open the car door for Kate. He went to the back of the car and placed his briefcase in the trunk before getting in the driver's seat.

There was little conversation along the way; they had long ago become comfortable being silent together as two introverts often are. They listened to a program on public radio about children whose biological fathers were sperm donors and the lengths these young adults were going to in order to find them. They both made a few noises about how they couldn't imagine being in that situation and about their hopes that the children would find closure. They drove into Georgetown and pulled into a parking garage.

The temperature had cooled down considerably now that the sun had set and Kate pulled her coat tightly around herself while fishing a pair of gloves out of her pocket. She wished she'd brought a hat. Brad seemed not to notice the cold and, while he wore his coat, he didn't button it or even put his bare hands in his pockets. They walked past the Brickskeller, a bar Kate had frequented as a graduate student, and continued deeper into Georgetown. They stopped at a restaurant whose sign simply read 'The Bistro'. Brad held the door while she entered, helped Kate off with her coat, removed his own, and handed both coats to the coat check attendant. After collecting the tickets, they put themselves on the restaurant's waitlist. With time to kill before they could be seated, Brad put his hand on the small of Kate's back and directed her toward the bar. "Let's have a drink. There's someone I want you to meet."

The room was crowded, but Brad managed to push his way to the bar with Kate in tow. He ordered a Scotch on the rocks and Kate asked for water, she didn't need any more alcohol today. Brad stretched to look over the crowd and when he saw who he was looking for, he waved. He took Kate's hand and pulled her along behind him emitting a string of "pardon me" and "excuse us" as he pushed through the crowd, holding his drink over his head like a beacon. They reached a gentleman who appeared to be in his 70s, balanced on a bar stool, holding a bourbon and clenching an unlit cigar in his teeth. "Good to see you Brad," the man mumbled moving only his lips so as not to lose the grip on his Padrón.

"Kate, I'd like you to officially meet Mr. Harry Clark. I believe the two of you have engaged in some correspondence."

Harry Clark removed the cigar from his mouth with his left hand while taking Kate's hand in his right. He kissed it. "Pleased to meet you, Dr. Adams", he said, "I'm sorry if I caused you any distress, or as the kids say, 'freaked you out'." He smiled an oversized smile that made his eyes squint and bowed his head. He struck Kate as a Texan by his grand gestures and carefully guarded accent.

"It's nice to finally meet you in person as well, Mr. Clark," Kate said politely while looking at Brad with a blank expression and then back to Mr. Clark with a forced smile. She was confused and somewhat apprehensive about why Brad had arranged the meeting.

"Kate, I still don't recommend doing business with this scoundrel," Brad said, aiming a friendly punch at Clark's shoulder, "but I wanted you to see he's not an enemy of the State. I know it's been bugging you. Would it be all right if he joined us for dinner?"

"Of course," Kate said, still stunned by the introduction.

"Oakley, party of three!" the hostess yelled into the bar. Brad had asked for a table for three, how had she missed that?

The hostess escorted them to a curved booth along the right-hand wall about two-thirds of the way into the dining room. Mr. Clark slid into the middle and rested his cigar on the table while Brad and Kate took the ends, with Brad facing the dining room door. The hostess handed them menus as oversized as Mr. Clark's smile.

"So, Mr. Clark, what brings you to The Bistro this evening?" Kate inquired coolly.

"Please, call me Harry and if it's all right I'd like to call you Kate," he suggested with another squinty-eyed grin, "It's not like we haven't already been acquainted," Kate nodded her approval

Brad chimed in, "It was my idea, Kate. When you called I was quite interested myself in what ol' Harry was up to. Really, I was most interested in ensuring he hadn't gone rogue on us." Brad forced a chuckle as he said it and Kate suspected he might not be kidding.

"Let me explain," Harry offered leaning back and folding his arms as the waiter arrived to take their drink order. Another scotch and bourbon were ordered for the men and Kate asked for a carafe of water. "I've been officially retired from the Agency now for almost fifteen years, but still work as a contractor. Yes, I do have a research think tank, but that is not the bulk of what I do personally. Brad wanted me to share what I do with you to put your mind at ease and shed some light on what was going on. I'm only authorized to tell you this because its been cleared by the Agency due to the security clearance you have for some of the consulting work you do for the SEC and Homeland, so consider us operating under those security guidelines." He had Kate's attention.

"Much of the work I do involves finding individuals with certain specific knowledge and, for lack of a better way of describing it, 'picking their brains'. I'm also involved with employee recruiting. Your knowledge of financial market structure, automated trading systems, and risk management put you on my radar. Frankly, after I had picked your brain for a while I was impressed, and had really hoped I'd be able to recruit you, but Brad set me straight on that." He grinned as Kate gave a quick snort.

Potential employment at the Agency had been a bone of contention during Kate and Brad's relationship. Kate had been considering joining the CIA after graduate school, but Brad was opposed. She recalled Brad saying he would be uncomfortable with many of the things Kate might be asked to do and that she had no idea what she was getting herself into. During one of their disagreements on the issue Brad had slammed his fist onto the kitchen counter to emphasize his point. It was the only time Kate had really seen him lose his cool.

By the end of their relationship she knew there was no way she could join the agency, she had seen firsthand what it did to people. Kate had always felt a bit sorry for Brad. He was a good man, with much to offer in a relationship, but would never be able to be truly intimate with anyone. He couldn't trust or let down his guard enough to let anyone else in. It always struck Kate as inconsistent that *he* was willing to engage in the agency's activities, while having a moral objection to her participating in them. Maybe he could only show affection through protection. Ultimately her decision not to join the agency was a good one, she could see Brad for who he was without becoming like him. She was probably happier than he was.

"Yes, a recruitment would have been an impossible task," Kate said, raising her glass in a mock toast.

"And now that that cat is out of the bag, let's get started on enjoying the rest of the evening," Harry said, picking up his menu in dramatic fashion "the steaks are excellent here, if you'd like my recommendation." Brad gave Kate a look from across the table that asked, "*Are we okay?*" Kate smiled and nodded; she appreciated his being forthright with her and also for getting Harry to stand down. She considered it an immeasurable favor. He didn't have to do it, but he did.

They did have an enjoyable evening. Harry entertained them with vivid storytelling that spanned his career at the agency, which had started shortly before the Cuban Missile Crisis. He was full of stories about colleagues, long since gone, and the funny things they did and said while under great stress during what had become significant events in American history. People in the Agency seemed to resort to gallows humor as a coping mechanism especially when they were hiding under desks in remote parts of the globe as people were shooting at them. He really should write a memoir, Kate thought. She would certainly read it.

Brad insisted on paying the bill, and the three of them walked together into the cold night air that now had light snow flurries swirling through it. Harry made a fresh clip on the end of his cigar, turned toward the building to avoid the wind, and lit it. He turned back toward Kate, grinning again with a look of satisfaction for an evening well done as smoke swirled around his head in competition with the flurries.

"My dear, it has indeed been a pleasure." Harry said, no longer trying too hard to suppress his Texas accent. He once again kissed Kate's hand and bowed. After shaking Brad's hand and saying goodnight he turned and walked in the opposite direction, waived his cigar-laden hand in the air and declaring loudly, "And the Republic stands!" Kate smiled. She genuinely liked Harry.

Kate and Brad returned to the parking garage to retrieve the car and laughed and chatted eagerly about Harry and his stories on the drive back to the hotel. Kate's day, that started so stressfully, was ending on a high note.

She was grateful. On the ride, Brad also offered to take Kate to breakfast in the morning and then drive her to the airport. Kate said it wouldn't be necessary, she could take the Metro, but he insisted. Kate was feeling too good to argue.

When they arrived at the hotel, the valet opened Kate's door and Brad got out, leaving the keys in the car and asking the valet to leave it running. He walked Kate inside where she made herself a cup of Chamomile tea from the lobby beverage station. Brad escorted her to the elevator where she turned to face him. "Thank you for a wonderful evening. I'll admit I had my doubts at first."

"It was fun" Brad replied, "and it was very nice to see you again after all these years". His eyes softened as he looked at Kate and took her hand. "You know, I could tell the valet to park the car so I can come upstairs with you. I am *very* good at keeping secrets". Kate felt a pang of desire in her stomach, but suppressed it quickly.

"You know I can't, Boo" she said.

"I know," Brad said, "but even though having sex with a married woman is outside my general moral code, there is something about you that makes me feel weak, vulnerable, and willing to compromise my principles. You're like Kryptonite to me. I don't suppose I can convince you we need to do it to for God and country?"

Kate took a step backwards and smiled, "What we have here is the tenacious force meeting the incorruptible object."

"Indeed", Brad said with a pained expression, "And that's probably a good thing". He said goodnight, hugged her and kissed her forehead. "I will see you in the morning."

Kate returned to the room and placed a video Skype call to Max in Singapore. He was having a great time with the students in Asia and both they and he were learning a lot. She filled him in on her day including Brad's proposition. "It sounds like I still win, so I'm happy", Max said knowing he had nothing to fear when it came to Kate's faithfulness. "It sounds like your day started out a bit rough, but I'm glad he was there to pull you out of it, especially since I couldn't be. I'll see you next week. I love you."

"I love you too, Max." They waved to each other and disconnected. It was the last time she would ever talk to him.

As she slept, there was a small explosion in the metro on the far side of the city. Kate was grateful she had Brad to drive her to the airport.

Chapter 6

May

Kate had finished grading the last of the semester's final exams and leaned back in her chair to watch the birds swarming the feeder in a small birch tree outside her campus office window. *Birds, cats, catbird, catbird seat, advantage, advantage Federer, tennis, racket, badminton, shuttlecock, rooster, birds.* Aha! Kate thought, a full circle.

The sun was shinning brightly this morning and the spring had been unusually warm for Alaska. It had been more than two weeks since she decided to give herself closure about Max's death and attempt to move forward. His passing had ignited a strong desire in Kate to work more diligently on a couple of research projects she had started before he disappeared including one on financial market security and another on the efficiencies of a variety of financial market structures. She had applied for and received two Federal grants for the studies and had requested a sabbatical during the upcoming academic year to work on them. Since her sabbatical had been granted, today would be her last day on campus until the fall semester of the following year. Fifteen months to isolate, heal, and immerse herself in work away from her critics. She wondered if it was too late to buy a yurt.

She poured some water from a gallon jug she kept under her desk into an electric kettle and went back to watching the birds. A squirrel had joined them and was running frantically up and down the tree trying to capture the sunflower seeds the birds were dropping on the ground. When the water boiled, Kate made herself a cup of green tea and turned back to the spring scene outside her window, placing her feet on the desk and reclining her chair. She was relaxed, content, and in no hurry to leave. Things were getting better.

"Hello, Kryptonite."

Kate spun around in her chair to find Brad leaning against the frame of her office door sipping coffee from a disposable cup encircled in a cardboard sleeve. Her look was one of genuine surprise as she went to hug him, careful not to spill her tea. "Hello, Boo! What are you doing here?" she asked.

She hadn't seen Brad since Max's memorial service, though he had called a few times since to see how she was doing. Kate had no reason to expect to see him in Alaska. He seemed pleased with himself for surprising her. "Do you have time for lunch?" he asked.

"But, it's only 10:00 in the morning", Kate said, looking at the clock above her door.

"I know, but I was hoping we could have lunch in Talkeetna and it will take us at least an hour and a half to get there."

Kate looked confused. "You want to have lunch in Talkeetna? Isn't that a little out of the way? What are you doing here anyway? While I can appreciate that Talkeetna has some great restaurants, isn't it is a bit far from DC for lunch?"

Talkeetna is a small historic town of less than 900 people near the base of the Alaska Range that features Denali, the highest mountain peak in North America. The views of the mountain range from Talkeetna are stunning and it is a popular tourist destination, but it is generally not a lunch choice for people living on the east coast.

"I'm here on a combination of business and pleasure. Taking a drive to see Denali and having lunch with you is the pleasure part. Interested?"

Kate starred at him momentarily unable to shake her confusion and then shook her head, threw her hands in the air and said, "Sure. Why the hell not." She grabbed her purse and jacket, locked her office door and the two of them headed for Brad's rented SUV.

They drove north on the Parks Highway and Brad chatted excitedly about Alaska, seeing moose near the airport and driving out to Eklutna Lake. He had been in the state for a little more than a week and between his 'business' he had managed to drive down the Kenai Peninsula to Soldotna, Hope, and Homer and even do a little hiking. She wished her business were more like his business, it seemed to involve a fair amount of recreation. But she was on sabbatical, who was she to judge. About that time they rounded a corner and went up a slight hill where the Big Mountain of Denali emerged in front of them. "Wow," said Brad, "It really is spectacular."

At the intersection of the Parks Highway and the Talkeetna Spur Road, they stopped at the combination gas station/convenience/liquor store/sandwich shop to use the restroom and grab some bottles of water before the fourteen-mile drive down the Talkeetna Spur Road into town. It was still early in the season, but Talkeetna was already bustling with tourists. They had to park about a mile outside of town in a State Park lot and walk in.

"I hear there's a restaurant here owned by a former White House chef," Brad said.

"That's true," confirmed Kate, "but that's not where I'm taking you."

There were no sidewalks in Talkeetna so they had to maneuver their way through the throng of people along the side of the road and Kate took Brad's arm so they wouldn't get separated. Several local dogs meandered down the middle of the street complicating the passing of cars on the narrow road. Kate pressed Brad down an alley and toward a local brewpub. They selected a table outside on the sprawling deck next to a young couple dining with their black lab at their feet. The dog looked up at them lazily as they approached before laying its head back down between its forepaws. Kate noticed Brad looking around the deck with a crooked smirk on his face.

"What?" asked Kate.

"I feel safer here than on a military base. So far I've counted five sidearms and those are just the open carries. There are probably at least as many concealed guns," Brad said with a laugh.

"Welcome to rural Alaska," Kate didn't mention the Ruger in her purse.

They looked at the beer menu and Kate ordered a Denali Single Engine Red, while Brad selected five beers for a sampler. They decided to share a Caesar salad and the halibut fish and chips and asked the server to bring some malt vinegar for the fish. Kate closed her eyes and turned her face toward the warm sun as she enjoyed the first sip of the cold, malty beer and its effervescence tickling her nose. She was reminded of the words of Walt Whitman 'Keep your face always toward the sunshine—and shadows will fall behind you.' Good advice. It was starting to feel like summer and she had a momentary sensation of relaxation once again.

Kate had started vegetable plants in the house the first week of March and in a few weeks it would be time to plant them outside, the thought of digging in the dirt calmed her. In her dreamy state of vegetable gardening she turned to Brad and asked, "How long are you staying?"

"Depends," he said with a shrug.

They shared their meal in relative silence, as Brad became engrossed in the people watching. He appeared amused as a group of tourists were paraded stiff-legged down Main Street encased in dry suits and helmets on their way to a white water rafting trip down the icy spring river. "If this were 20,000 Leagues Under the Sea, all those people would parish in a giant squid attack with only Captain Nemo living to tell the tale," Brad mused. "I get why you live here, this place is great."

Following lunch they made their way back down the alley and across the street to Nagley's Store for ice cream cones. They had consumed their ice cream by the time they reached the SUV. As they started back down the Talkeetna Spur Road, Brad turned to Kate, "As long as we're this far, if you can spare a couple more hours, I'd like to show you something."

Kate looked at him through squinted eyes, "Is this still part of the 'pleasure' portion of your trip?"

"I guess we'll find out," Brad replied.

As they turned north onto the Parks Highway, Brad handed Kate a manila envelope and said, "By the way, your security clearance has been both renewed and upgraded. The protocols are in the envelope. I'd appreciate if you would read them while we drive, where I'm taking you falls under them".

Kate squinted at him again and opened the envelope and began reading the contents. *Fascinating*, she thought. She had applied for a renewal of her security clearance with her grant applications, as she needed access to financial market data that required it, but she certainly hadn't expected it to come from Brad.

After about fifty minutes they turned left onto an unmarked gravel road. Kate knew the area as Trapper Creek. Many of the roads in the area were only accessible in the summer and were not plowed or otherwise maintained in the winter. It made the area a destination for recreational 4-wheeling in the summer and snowmachining in the winter. Its remote location and lack of labeled roads and trails made it primarily a place used by Alaskans, it was too far off the beaten path for tourists. If you went far enough into the Trapper Creek area you ran into an area abundant with small gold mining operations, not to mention people living in trucks, trailers, and motorhomes in order to evade law enforcement.

Trapper Creek was as close as you could get to the Wild West. If you were hiding from the law you could still usually get a job that paid cash at one of the gold mines and you could get fed, at least during the summer, at a small roadhouse on one of the mines that served lunch and dinner to mine owners and their employees. If you caused trouble, you might end up dead. Gold miners were a paranoid lot and didn't appreciate outsiders encroaching on their territory. If Brad was impressed by the concentration of firearms in Talkeetna he should wander onto a mining claim. They might even let him look down the barrel of one.

The gravel road met the quality control standards of a washboard. They went up and down over hump after hump for about 20 miles and finally turned left on a narrow graveled trail. It was still early spring in Alaska and patches of snow remained visible in the grass along the sides of the road and the melting snow made the gravel roads wet and soft. The trail they had turned onto had considerably less gravel and more mud with deep water and slush-filled potholes. Kate thought she may have dislodged a kidney as they were tossed around vigorously even at a slow rate of speed. They would have been better off if they had parked in the gravel lot about two miles back and taken a 4-wheeler down the trail she thought, but city boys don't think of these things.

After only a few miles, though it was significantly farther if you added the vertical distance traveled, they turned right onto an overgrown path that showed the slightest trace of past tire tracks. Tree branches scraped the rented SUV as they drove about a mile to a clearing. To the left was a padlocked gate in front of what appeared to be a gravel driveway; to the right was a large pond. There was no need to attach a fence to the gate, the trees and dead winter vegetation were so thick, there would be no way to drive a vehicle onto the property without using the road. Brad hopped out of the SUV, unlocked the gate, and swung it to the left and used the chain and lock to attach it to a tree to hold it open.

They drove down the narrow, graveled lane for about a quarter of a mile until they reached another clearing. To their right was an outbuilding with weathered vertical siding that more closely resembled a large shed than a garage. On the side was a double door about the size of a small garage door with a wooden ramp approaching it. Attached to the shed was a large lean-to divided into two sections. On the right was split and stacked firewood stacked two deep, while the left side contained wood that had yet to be split. An axe was struck into a large stump next to the structure implying this was where wood was split.

Ahead of them was a two-story cedar-sided cabin about twenty-four feet by thirty-six, that sat on a six foot high concrete foundation. The height of the foundation indicated the cabin was designed for year-round use. In this part of Alaska it was not unusual to have more than four feet of snow on the ground during the winter and cabins were often built high so they didn't have to be perpetually dug out. The cabin had a green metal peaked roof with a wooden ladder attached on each side of the peak. The ladders made it easier to walk on the roof in the winter to remove snow. If you didn't shovel the snow off, the weight could collapse the roof. The roof extended out over a deck that wrapped around the cabin with a large screened porch on half the deck facing the drive. The main entrance included an arctic entryway.

Near the cabin was a small building that Kate guessed was the power house, where the generators and/or battery banks were stored that provided electricity to cabins that were remote and off-grid. There was a large solar panel in the yard, so there was at least a battery bank, but to provide power in the winter usually required a generator to serve as backup. Alongside the power house was a large raspberry patch.

A pole about fifty feet high was attached to the side of the cabin and topped with what looked like a thick, hard plastic flag. Kate recognized it as a cell phone range extender designed to capture the signal from a distant cell tower to allow the use of cell phones at a remote location. There was another, shorter pole that contained an oblong shaped satellite dish pointed toward the distant ground. The relative position of Alaska on the planet meant that satellites in the Alaskan sky are located near the horizon as opposed to other parts of the country where they are up in the sky. In the far corner of the yard was an outhouse that appeared to be wrapped in Christmas lights. Brad parked near a fire pit that had been built near the cabin and they got out of the SUV.

"What do you think?" Brad asked.

As Kate walked toward the cabin, she noticed it had a spectacular view of the foothills of the Alaska Range with the Denali and Foraker peaks rising up behind them. They were much closer to the mountain range here than they were in Talkeetna. She noticed how absolutely quiet it was except for the sounds of birds she couldn't see and a river running in the distance. "It's a wonderful spot, but if you've been out here, I'm guessing today wasn't the first time you saw the mountains," Kate said with a sideways glance.

"Not true, when I was out here before it was cloudy and I couldn't see them. Let's go inside." He tugged her toward the door.

Brad unlocked the door and they stepped into the arctic entryway. The wall against the cabin was lined with open wooden lockers with a series of hooks and pegs inside and a shelf at the top of each. The narrow walls on the sides of the entry contained cabinets under small windows, while the outside wall just to the right of the door had a board attached to the floor with long pegs sticking up designed to hold inverted wet or muddy boots. There was a row of pegs for coats above it. To the left of the door were windows and a long bench. The entryway was covered in a large outdoor, water-absorbing mat with a rubber back designed to dry quickly. "We can leave our shoes here," Brad said slipping off the heel of his left shoe with the toe of his right. Kate kicked off her Danskos and tucked them under the bench.

Brad unlocked the interior cabin door and the two them stepped up onto the hardwood floor. From the door Kate could see the far wall of the cabin had windows that looked out on the mountain range, between them was a large, black, wood-burning stove. There was no electricity currently on in the cabin, but the windows let in enough light to see clearly. To their left was a kitchen with hickory cabinets, a small cabin-sized range and refrigerator, and a stackable washer and dryer. Kate noticed there were also a dishwasher and a sink. This was unusual because most cabins in the area are considered 'dry' because they didn't have running water. "Water?" Kate asked pointing to the sink.

"Yes, there is a well on the property."

This was confirmed when Kate looked to her right and saw a small bathroom that included a shower stall. Ahead of her was a dining area with a round oak table beyond which was the great room. There was a breakfast bar at the intersection of the kitchen and great room and adjacent to it was a bumped out area that contained stairs that went both up to the second floor and down to the basement area in the foundation.

In addition to the view and wood stove, the great room contained a center seating area with a coffee table; two buffalo leather recliners, and a sofa in a durable-looking burgundy fabric. There was also a corner desk with a computer, a wall-mounted television, and two chairs with a small table against the wall opposite the stairs. Beside the chairs was a door that went out to the screened section of the deck. Brad continued, "The oddly shaped satellite dish you saw outside provides both Internet and satellite television." Kate guessed it was probably the only cabin in the area that had either of those amenities.

The walls and ceilings were cedar tongue and groove and there were two large ceiling fans, one over the great room and one over the dining area. They proceeded upstairs where they found themselves on a landing that was used as a workout area with a treadmill, universal gym, and some free weights. The walls were lined with bookshelves, packed with books. There was one large bedroom overlooking the mountains and two smaller ones, both with built-in bunk beds. The large bedroom had a queen-sized bed topped with a downed comforter covered in a quilt, an armoire, and a desk. The wall over the desk was covered with a whiteboard that included some colorful, round magnets in the upper right-hand corner. There was also a small bathroom with a tub on the second floor and another door that was locked. "What's in here?" Kate asked pointing at the door.

"A small room used for storage, but I don't have that key with me," Brad replied.

"The cabin is very nice and I love the location, but why did you bring me here?" Kate asked.

"Let's go downstairs and sit down," Brad suggested as he took Kate's arm and guiding her toward the stairs.

They sat next to each other on the leather sofa and Kate noticed it had a pullout bed underneath.

Brad took a deep breath and looked Kate in the eyes, "Kate, I have a proposition that I think will benefit both of us," he looked at his hands and rubbed them together before looking back at Kate. "You are going on sabbatical to do some research and I know you have a desire to isolate and step away from it all for a little while and I would like to offer you this cabin as a place to do that, but there is a catch." Kate sat up a little straighter bracing for what might be coming next.

"We use this cabin as a safe house of sorts. Generally, it's a place where we bring some people returning from overseas assignments to lay low for a while…you know…hide out until the excitement they've been involved in dies down a bit." Kate was shifting in her seat, "I need someone who is familiar with the area and living in remote Alaska to run it for me for a while, and I hoped you would be willing to do it. Just through the winter."

Kate bolted to a standing position and yelled, "Are you fucking insane!" in a tone of voice that made her uncomfortable when she heard it. She dialed it back a bit, "Why on earth would I want to do that? Why would *you* want me to do it? Didn't we have this conversation years ago? I seem to recall you want me as far away from your work as possible, not dropped in the middle of people who have recently experienced 'excitement'!" She provided air quotes to emphasize 'excitement'. A flood of long buried resentment toward Brad enveloped her. He was always trying to tell her what to do. She paced in a circle. "What exactly is it about this particular assignment that makes you suddenly want me involved?"

"Well, first of all we're talking about a temporary assignment. Second, it's a safe house so there's not exactly a lot of danger here, but there is one more thing." Brad seemed calm, but once again looked at his hands as if he were trying to maintain his composure, "We have come into possession of some of the materials recovered during the investigation of Max's death. If you do this…if you are working for us as a contractor…I can give you access to those materials, but only on this secure property. It might help you get some real closure. I might also be able to help you get better access to the data you need for your research."

"Dammit, Brad!", Kate shouted. She had been so close to moving on, letting it go, but now the anxiety of not knowing how Max had died was once again welling up inside of her. The emotions were still too close to the surface, she hadn't buried them deeply enough yet. Would knowing more make it easier or more difficult for her set aside Max's death? Kate sat down heavily on the sofa and put her face in her hands "I need to think about it."

"There's no time to think about it, I need to know now."

Dammit, dammit, dammit! Kate wanted to cry, but was too angry. Removing her hands she looked back at Brad, "I have some conditions."

"Tell me," he said.

CHAPTER 7

Two weeks later, Kate and Brad were at a Palmer, Alaska garden center collecting a load of topsoil in Kate's pickup truck. The truck was also pulling a small enclosed trailer that contained luggage, a few boxes, and the plants for her vegetable garden that she had originally been planning for her own home. After loading the dirt into the truck's bed, they headed north on the Parks Highway toward Talkeetna. They pulled into the parking lot of the Talkeetna hardware store around noon. Kate had reserved a rototiller at the store, but it wouldn't be ready until after lunch, so Kate suggested they walk across the street for a pizza. After lunch they walked into the hardware store where a man in his mid thirties wearing Carhartt coveralls greeted Kate and Brad as they entered the store. He sported an Ace hardware baseball cap atop prematurely graying, shoulder-length hair. When he smiled his long, bushy beard nearly consumed his mouth. He gave Brad one of those up and down looks that showed he knew that Brad was not from around there.

He moved closer to Kate, "Ma'am, what can I help you find today." Kate had been identified as the local, probably due to the .357 snub nose Ruger resting in a leather holster under Kate's shoulder. It would be her constant companion now that she was going to be living in an area where bears outnumbered people three to one, not to mention the occasional encounter with a skittish gold miner. The Ruger wasn't great for distance, but would penetrate a bear's skull at close range. She had a Winchester Model 94 in the truck in case she needed to defend herself, or someone else, from a greater distance.

"Well, Cody," Kate said looking at his nametag, "I reserved a rototiller for a three day rental and was told it would be ready after lunch today. I hope I'm not too early. It's reserved under the name Kate Adams."

"Not at all ma'am, I'll bring it around to the front of the store." Cody left to find the tiller.

Kate walked outside to a tent where the hardware store's summer garden department had been set up. She selected two trays of flowers that included razor grass, daisies, and petunias and two large, round plastic flowerpots. She also selected some basil, sage, thyme, rosemary, and several dill plants. They finished paying for the plants and tiller rental just as Cody returned with the machine. Brad loaded it into the trailer, while Kate placed the plants on the floor of the truck's backseat, wedging them in tightly using boxes and rolled up towels and blankets so they wouldn't be upended during the ride down the rough roads to the cabin. Kate waved to Cody as they drove away.

The safe house would not be active for another week to ten days, but Kate wanted some time to get settled. One of her conditions for taking the assignment was that Brad help her create the vegetable garden she had planned to plant in her own yard, which was no easy task in remote Alaska. The land the cabin stood on had been relatively untouched by humans until recent years and as a result it had about four feet of hard, decomposed plant material sitting over the topsoil. Walking on the ground felt a bit like an extra-firm mattress—springy, but not soft. They would need to use pickaxes and chainsaws to cut through the layer of organic material, till the hard ground beneath it, and then add the topsoil from the truck to build it back up to ground level. A strong, six-foot tall wire fence would then need to be built both around and over the garden to keep the local wildlife out while letting the sun in. It would be easier to build raised beds, but root vegetables like potatoes and carrots would need the insulation of the ground during the cold summer nights.

The previous week Kate had spent three days at the cabin with two agents from the Agency and three Air Force officers from Joint Base Elmendorf-Richardson who would be coordinating guests and supplies. She learned about operating the power and other systems at the cabin and diligently typed scheduled routine maintenance events like changing water filters and cleaning solar panels into her phone's calendar so she would be electronically reminded.

On this second trip she was taken into the large shed and shown that it contained a small shop with a large selection of tools, two ATVs, and two snowmachines that would carry two people each, and a small tow behind trailer for an ATV and a towable sled for a snowmachine. There was also a riding lawnmower and a snowplow blade that would fit on an ATV. On the second day, Kate and the Air Force officers boarded the ATVs and rode down a trail about two miles into a heavily wooded area where they stopped and asked Kate what she saw. "Trees," she said. They smirked, and pulled back some brush to reveal a gate in a chain link fence with vine-like weeds growing through it. They walked through the gate and onto a well-hidden grass airstrip. "This is why you need a lawnmower and a snow plow," explained one of the officers.

"Wow," said Kate, "I don't know how I'm going to keep up with all of this and still get my research done!"

"Don't worry," the officer said, "your guests are required to do most of the heavy labor. The last thing we need are testosterone-infused men stuck in the middle of nowhere with nothing to do. You are the manager, they provide the labor. Your main priority is your academic work. You'll even find that some of them are so happy to be in a safe, homey location that they want to cook."

"Things are looking up!" Kate said.

They returned to the cabin where Kate was taken upstairs to the locked storage room Brad had not opened for her. When the door was opened she understood why. The small windowless room, not much bigger than a large walk-in closet, was a communication center. While there was cell phone service available via the range extender antenna, it was to be used only as a last resort and would not generally be powered. Tracking cell phones was too easy and other methods of communication and coded messages would be utilized. The room contained a secure satellite phone, a laptop computer, and short-wave radio equipment. Kate was told that the room was to be considered a secure area and guests were never to enter it. "We can't risk discovery because a guest decides he wants to call his or her family," warned one of the agents. If someone were trying to reach her via the satellite phone, a buzzer would sound both inside and outside the cabin to alert her, email alerts would show up on her cell phone, which would be connected to the secure Wi-Fi network. The rest of their work that day involved learning how to use the equipment and additional ways messages would be transmitted and how they would be coded. It was an intense day and by the time they sat down to eat the military MREs the Air Force had provided, Kate was exhausted.

The third day was spent reviewing code and working on Kate's supply list. There was a chest freezer in the power house and it needed to be stocked as the number of guests present at any one time was uncertain. The Air Force would be supplying fresh milk, juice, eggs, fruit, vegetables, meat, and gasoline weekly. In an emergency the basement was stocked with MREs, extra fuel, and water. There was a large propane tank on the property that fueled the stove, refrigerator, chest freezer, and washer/dryer that would be refilled just before snowfall and should last throughout the winter. In addition to the woodstove for heat, the cabin had a Toyostove—a heater that uses a small amount of fuel oil to provide heat—as a secondary heat source that could be set thermostatically to keep the cabin at a somewhat steady temperature when the woodstove was not tended during the night or when they were working outside.

Today Kate and Brad arrived at the cabin once again after a long, bumpy ride. The day was overcast and the cheery quaintness she had felt the first time they visited was replaced by a sense of oppressiveness. It took Kate a minute to catch her breath as she stepped out of the truck and recovered from a jolt of anxiety. "You can do this Kate", she muttered under her breath.

Brad unlocked the cabin and they did a quick walkthrough. The food supplies had been stocked and an inventory sheet was left on the dining room table along with instructions about how to maintain the inventory list. They rolled the tiller off the trailer, neatly lined the plants up in a sunny spot in the yard, and began hauling boxes and suitcases into the cabin. Kate had brought her own linens, even though the cabin was fully stocked with them. There were some things the government should never be trusted with and linens were one of those things.

Kate went out and turned on the solar power supply, and made sure the pressure tank was full of water. They turned on a few lights to counteract the gloominess of the day and Kate went into the communication center and powered on the computer, satellite dish, Wi-Fi, and shortwave radio and plugged the satellite phone into its charger and turned it on. They both logged their phones into the Wi-Fi network. "I guess we have no more excuses for not starting the garden project," Brad lamented.

On her previous visit, Kate had marked the spot for her garden with stakes and rope. It was near where they had set the plants and about 10 feet from the cabin. There were two chainsaws in the shed and they had brought an extra bar and chain for each, as they would have to be replaced after "digging" the garden.

Kate took the smaller of the two chainsaws and between the two of them they cut a grid pattern of one-foot squares in the 6 by 7 foot garden. Then, they each took pickaxes and shovels and started pulling the material out of the garden. After about three and a half hours they were both ready to quit for the day. The mosquitoes and biting gnats were getting thicker as the afternoon wore on and they had doused themselves in so much bug spray they were beginning to repel each other. They went inside where Brad found some lemonade concentrate in the freezer, added some water and poured a glass for each. They sat at the table sipping lemonade and talking about the plan for tomorrow's gardening until their limp arms recovered enough that they felt they could wash themselves in a shower.

After she showered, Kate came down dressed in pajamas and fixed two plates with sandwiches of ham lettuce, tomato, and spicy mustard and apple slices. Brad emerged from the downstairs bathroom dressed in athletic shorts and a Wisconsin Badgers sweatshirt. Kate rummaged through the cabinets until she found a package of Oreo cookies that would have to suffice as dessert. Brad grabbed the plates, put the package of Oreos under his arm, and took their dinner to the table as Kate filled two glasses with ice and water.

"Do you want a beer?" she asked.

"No thank you," Brad replied, "I think water will be enough tonight."

Kate turned on the radio in the dining area that was set to the Talkeetna radio station to listen to the news. Every night after the news, the radio station transmitted messages for people living in remote parts of the listening area that didn't have phone service or other means of communication.

"I have a message for Petersville Joe," the announcer said, "We hope you're well, your sister had her baby Tuesday, it's a girl. They named her Angela Marie, 7 lbs, 6 ozs. We hope you can get to town to see her soon. Keep your socks dry. Love Mom, Dad, Fran, Bud, and Angela"

"To Frank and Lila, supplies on their way tomorrow. Tried to fly in today, but the pass closed up. Over and out."

"To Crabber Bob, stuck at Judy's place. One of those stupid water rodents built a dam in the creek and flooded the yard. She won't let me leave. I'll be spending tomorrow thwarting Judy's beaver." Brad choked a little on his sandwich as he, Kate, *and* the announcer went into fits of teary-eyed laughter.

"Well," Brad said when he regained some composure, "it's good to have a plan." More laughter followed that comment.

"I've missed you Kate. It's been nice working and laughing with you again," Brad said when he managed to stop laughing.

"Yes it has," Kate replied with a smile while standing and beginning to clear the empty plates, "Would you like some tea or coffee to go with your Oreos?"

"I'll have whatever you're having, but let me wash the dishes while you fix it." Brad followed Kate to the kitchen where he found a dish drainer under the sink and set it up on the counter while he ran hot water into the sink. Kate filled the teakettle from the running water and placed it on the stove to boil. She removed two mugs from a cupboard and peppermint teabags from another. Brad was finished with the dishes before Kate had steeped the tea. He waited at the dining room table until Kate arrived with the tea and a couple of napkins to put their cookies on. Brad suggested they try out the satellite television after dinner to see if it was worth the government's extra expense.

Brad grabbed the remote control for the television and sat in one of the buffalo hide recliners. Kate lay on the couch and rested her head on a tapestry throw pillow. She was beginning to feel her exhaustion and the muscles in her lower back were twitching rhythmically from the day's exertion. Brad spent the next fifteen minutes adjusting the various options on the television from the aspect ratio to color saturation. Once he discovered the cabin had surround sound he experimented with different sound formats. Kate just wondered why a remote cabin would be equipped with surround sound and fantasized about ways to reduce government spending. They settled on a movie that involved an art thief and the journalist trying to catch him, but Kate remembered little of it as she dozed in and out of sleep on the couch. At 10:00 she got up, kissed Brad on the top of the head and said goodnight, then stumbled up the stairs and into bed.

CHAPTER 8

Kate was an early riser and usually woke between five and six to catch up on overnight news and email. She was one of those annoying morning people who woke up refreshed and ready to go, so she was surprised when the clock read 7:30 the next morning when she woke up and she was still feeling lethargic. *All this fresh air is killing me,* she thought as she rubbed her neck and became aware of the sounds of Brad moving around downstairs. No matter how early Kate woke up, she never seemed to get up before Brad and she was starting to suspect he never slept. When she pulled back the covers, she noticed the cabin had gotten quite cold overnight; she pulled her robe on over her pajamas and put on her slippers before she walked downstairs. Brad was once again in his shorts, sweatshirt, and bare feet pulling eggs and bacon out of the refrigerator. "Aren't you cold?" Kate asked still wearing the stunned look of someone who, while up, was not quite 'at 'em.'

"Good morning to you too," Brad replied with a smile and a peck on the cheek, "Coffee has been made and if you will grab a couple of potatoes out of the pantry I'll add hash browns to our breakfast. Didn't you used to be a morning person? I thought for a while there I was going to have to bring you breakfast in bed." Kate offered a sarcastic laugh while opening the pantry door, thinking she should probably have coffee before trying to formulate witty retorts.

It took the two of them another day and a half to pull out the layers of decomposing plant material, till the soil, and fill it with topsoil. Kate saved some of the topsoil to put in the two planters she had placed on either side of the cabin door and filled them with the annuals she had purchased at the hardware store. It was a nice touch that made the place look a little more like a home. Most of the herbs she bought were inside on the dining table, but she would save some room for the sage and dill in the garden.

Around noon on the third day they got back in the truck and started the two-hour drive back to Talkeetna to return the rented tiller. With the tiller returned, Brad asked, "So what else would you like to do before you are sequestered in the cabin?"

This would be Kate's last trip out for the better part of a year and she swallowed hard at the thought. They spent the afternoon like tourists roaming the streets of the village. They made a trip to the small museum that documented the history of the local area and some of its more notorious characters, a gold panning lesson, and a trip to a bazaar set up in a local park. As 5:00 approached a band began setting up on a small stage in the park. Brad and Kate found a picnic table and 30 minutes later a bluegrass band began playing and a crowd gathered. They engaged in clapping, foot stomping, and singing along when the band prompted all the while smiling and laughing. At one point Brad even briefly held Kate's hand. She didn't stop him. They finished the evening with dinner and a couple of glasses of wine at the Wildflower Grill.

They drove back to the cabin singing along with songs on a classic rock station and reminiscing about what their lives were like and the things they were doing at the time the songs were popular. It was an evening to remember.

When they arrived at the cabin, there was a moose sniffing Kate's annuals in hopes that the flowers might make a tasty snack. A few blasts of the truck's horn discouraged the thought and moved the moose along, but not before it sent a threatening sideways glance and a kick of its hind leg their way in protest. The inside of the cabin was cool and dim, but there was a lingering scent of the previous night's chicken dinner, which added warmth. "Cake?" Kate asked.

"Not for me," Brad said, "I've eaten too much and I'm kind of tired."

Kate felt similarly, but was reluctant to let the evening end. She fixed herself a cup of chamomile tea to help her wind down. When she emerged from the kitchen, Brad met her in the dining area with the soft look in his eyes she'd seen before. He took the mug from her hand, set it on the table and wrapped his strong arms around her, hugging her tightly and lingering longer than usual. When he released her, he gave her a long kiss on the forehead and said, "Goodnight Kryptonite. We'll start the fence in the morning." He turned and walked up the stairs as Kate grabbed a chair to steady herself.

A

The sun shining in her eyes awakened Kate the next morning. While there was little darkness this time of year, the previously cloudy sky had been muting the impact of the summer sun. She would have to remember to close the blinds before bed. To no one's surprise, Brad was already up, sipping coffee in the recliner, and reading a book about the history of European conflict when Kate came downstairs. "Good morning, Boo," she said walking past his chair and touching him briefly on the shoulder as she passed.

"Good morning," Brad replied with a stretch, before going back to his book.

Kate filled a mug with coffee and sliced off a piece of cake before moving to the dining table. "Will it bother you if I turn on the radio?" she asked Brad. She might as well get into the habit, listening to the radio in the morning and early evening would be part of her job.

"Not at all, I need to get up and eat something anyway. What do you have there, cake? That's a fabulous idea, breakfast of champions isn't it?"

"It's at least the breakfast of remote fence builders."

The radio droned on in the background with a program featuring local buy, sell, and swap ads. As Brad arrived at the table with his cake, with an added scoop of ice cream, the morning message announcements started.

"To Out There Jane", Kate set her fork down when she recognized her radio code name, "We would like to fly in today around 4 with a guest for dinner. Realize its short notice, but taking a chance that you're around and not out hunting or fishing."

Brad read her face, "Is that for you?" Kate nodded. "Are you ready for guests?"

"Well, I have to start sometime. Maybe he or she can help us build a fence," Kate said with every ounce of optimism she could muster.

"Then I guess you're in business." As he said it, the buzzer sounded alerting Kate to a satellite call and she ran upstairs to the communication room to answer it.

She returned to the dining room, "They were concerned I wouldn't hear the radio broadcast since I'm not officially on duty yet. Looks like my first guest will only be here for about four weeks, but they tell me I'm also going to have a long-term guest who will be arriving sometime within the next few weeks."

"Welcome to The Firm," Brad said raising his mug so they could toast the occasion.

They spent the rest of the morning working on the fence. After lunch Kate decided if a plane was coming in, she should probably mow the airstrip, as the grass would have grown enough to cut just in the time they'd been there. In Alaska, the 24-hour sun meant you had to cut your grass every three days or so. Brad stayed behind to work on the fence.

Kate felt out of place driving a riding lawnmower down an ATV trail in remote Alaska. *No one would ever think she was up to something unusual,* she thought sarcastically. While the lawnmower was all-wheel-drive, the trail was challenging and full of ruts and tree roots making it difficult to get the mower to the field. About halfway there she decided that if she got the mower to the airstrip, it was going to stay there. She'd come back later with a tarp to cover it with.

Once she finally arrived, it took almost two hours to cut and bag the thick, tall grass and Kate was covered in dust and grass when she finished. She was just brushing the grass off the lawnmower when Brad arrived on an ATV. He looked at her covered in dirt and debris and laughed, "I knew fence building was the better job. You seemed like you were gone for quite a long time so I thought I'd check on you. We'll have company in less than an hour."

"Shower. Now." Kate said with a sneeze as she climbed on the back of the ATV.

With her hair still damp from the shower and wearing clean clothes, Kate came outside to check on Brad. He was taking a break, drinking lemonade, and holding a level against a fencepost. "Plumb," he said with pride and Kate swore he stuck his chest out a bit.

"I'm heading up to the airstrip to pick up our guest, do you want to ride along?"

"No. Your job take in boarders, mine build fence," he said in his best Tarzan voice while thumping his chest one time, "Although, for the record, fence building does underutilize my superior spy skills."

Kate rolled her eyes and headed for the shed where she grabbed a tarp for the mower and hooked the small tow-behind trailer to the ATV. The trip down the trail was much easier now that she was not on a lawnmower and she arrived at the field before the plane, giving her time to wrap the mower in the blue tarp. At 4:00 sharp, a small bush plane rolled onto the landing strip and came to a stop near Kate.

The pilot jumped out and the passenger-side door opened. The pilot ran around to help the passenger out of the plane. The guest looked to be in some discomfort and he leaned on the pilot as they walked toward Kate and the ATV.

"Murphy," the man said offering his hand to shake, "friends call me Murph."

"I'm Kate, it's nice to meet you Murph," she said taking his offered hand.

At the safe house, no one would ever know anyone's full name. Only first or last names, never both; Kate didn't ask Murphy which his was. Murphy was about five feet ten inches of pure muscle and had an olive completion, longish black hair, and about a six inch beard. It was no mystery to Kate where this man had been experiencing his 'excitement'. His accent implied he was originally from Brooklyn or maybe the Bronx, the nuances of New York accents always eluded Kate.

The pilot spoke, "Murph here took a bullet to his right leg, but the bullet went through and didn't hit anything important…well…except his leg of course. They've patched him up, but he's going to need rest and help with bandage changes. Oh, and make sure he takes his antibiotic.

I guess he won't be building any fences, Kate thought. "I'll take good care of him," Kate said.

"Get him on your ATV and standby, I've got his gear and some packages that need to be delivered," the pilot ordered.

Murphy winced as Kate helped him throw his leg across the back seat of the ATV. She then climbed on herself while the pilot loaded the trailer.

The pilot placed a large duffle bag that presumably belonged to Murphy and a metal box with a locked lid that was slightly larger than a crate into the trailer. He handed Kate a sealed padded envelope and said, "The box and the envelope are for Mr. Oakley, will you make sure he gets them and confirms their arrival?"

"I will," Kate said tucking the envelope between her leg and the seat.

Kate and Murphy waited until the plane was safely in the air before beginning the journey to the cabin. Kate drove slowly to minimize the jarring of Murphy's leg, but he often made muffled noises of pain. As they were pulling up, Brad pealed himself away from the cabin where he was leaning to admire his work on the fence and began to mosey in their direction. As Kate started helping Murphy off the ATV, Brad could see he was injured and quickened his pace to help. They got him into the cabin and onto the couch, where Kate propped some pillows behind him.

"While I know there is no good answer to this question, are you comfortable?" Kate asked hopefully.

"As comfortable as I can get," Murphy replied through gritted teeth. "Hi, I'm Murphy, but you can call me Murph."

As Brad opened his mouth to respond, Kate jumped in. "That's Mr. Oakley." If he had introduced himself as Brad, Murphy would know his full name.

"Yes," Brad said nodding with a curious look on his face, "Call me Oakley."

"Mr. Oakley, the duffle bag in the trailer belongs to Murph, but the box and this are deliveries for you," Kate said handing the envelope with "Oakley" written on it to Brad. He nodded again and seemed to understand why she was suddenly calling him Mr. Oakley. "You are to confirm their arrival."

"Thanks," Brad said while raising his eyebrows to Kate and feigning a sigh of relief that she had prevented him from introducing himself as Brad.

"Murph, you rest there. Mr. Oakley will take your things to your room and I'll go get dinner started," Kate said, but Murphy's eyes were already getting heavy.

Kate retired to the kitchen to work on a beef stew and biscuits, and Brad brought in the duffel and box, and put them on Murphy's bunk and the communications room respectively. Brad closed and locked the door while in the communications room, probably to confirm the arrival of the packages.

"The fence is finished and it looks like tomorrow is my last full day here. I'll be leaving the following day on the supply plane that will be arriving at 1:00. Something smells good." Brad announced as he entered the kitchen. He leaned over Kate's shoulder with his hands on her hips to look into the pot of beef stew she was stirring.

"Step away from the stove," Kate said playfully, "I have hot liquid here and I'm not afraid to use it." Brad laughed, stepped back and leaned against the counter.

"Are you going to be all right out here by yourself? I realize things got started sooner than you expected."

"Of course I will, Mr. Oakley. I was by myself before I got here and I can probably survive once again without you." Kate's voice had a hint of sharpness to it. He was always so protective. She knew she was a perfectly capable and competent woman, why didn't he?

They heard some movement coming from the great room and looked around the corner to see what was going on. Murphy was sitting on the edge of the couch stretching and starting to pull himself into a standing position. "Are you all right over there?" Brad asked.

"Yeah," Murphy said straightening himself into an upright position, "They gave me some pain pills to make the trip easier, but frankly I'd rather feel some pain, if it means I still have my wits about me. I feel better now that the meds have worn off." He was walking stiff-legged toward the kitchen while holding on to the furniture and walls. "I could stand a drink of water though." His accent making 'though' sound like 'dough'. Brad showed him where the glasses and ice were and Murphy made it himself. Brad looked at Kate as if to say *don't wait on him, let him do it for himself* and Murphy seemed to expect to do so. Kate suggested Murphy take a seat at the table, as dinner would be ready soon. She looked at Brad, "Mr. Oakley, since I'm not supposed to wait on people, I believe it is your turn to set the table. And turn the radio on if you would, please."

"Damn, that's good," Murphy exclaimed after taking a few bites of his stew and ripping off a piece of buttered biscuit with his teeth, "Somethin' about a homemade meal almost makes a guy think he's gonna be awright, 'cha know." His New York accent slurred his words together somewhat.

"Thank you," said Kate politely.

"So how are things over there, Murph?" Brad asked generically.

"They suck, man. Everywhere you turn there's another group of 10 or 20 people tryin' ta cut your head off. They're fuckin' nuts and I don't know how they put up with these fuckin' beards." Murph scratched his beard vigorously. "I try to blend in, but if you're my age and not part of a roving gang of head choppers, they come after you too, even if you're one of 'em. Makes the gangs in the Bronx look like pussies, I can tell ya that. I say, to hell with 'em, build a fence and let 'em kill each other." He waved his biscuit for emphasis.

They ate silently for a few minutes listening to the news on the radio. "I guess I don't really mean that," Murphy said, "I'd rather kill them myself first. Dirtbags." Obviously, Murph had a few things to work through.

Brad added, "Hang in there, we'll get 'em and you'll be a big part of it." Kate wondered if that was the standard retention cheer, maybe she should have brought pom poms.

After dinner, Murphy said if Brad and Kate would bring the dishes in, he felt well enough to load the dishwasher. When Murphy exited the kitchen, Brad was reclined watching a Cubs game in glorious surround sound and Kate was wiping off the dining table.

"And the women," Murph said approaching Kate, "I haven't seen anything but a woman's eyes in six months. You my dear are a sight for sore eyes. When I'm well enough..." He wrapped his arms around Kate from behind, pressed his body firmly against her and started kissing her neck. Brad jumped up from his chair just as Kate grabbed Murphy's pinky finger and bent it backwards causing him to release his grip and fall to his knees as Kate turned to face him. Seeing she had things well in hand, Brad slowly sat back down in his chair.

"Don't you ever do that to me again!" Kate shouted, "I am here to run a safe house, not for my guests to play patty cake with! Do you understand me, Murph?!" She placed an emphasis on Murph.

"Yes, ma'am," Murphy said sheepishly, grimacing in pain. Kate released his finger. "I think I'll go unpack my things now." He used a chair to pull himself up and staggered toward the stairs.

"I'll help you," Brad offered following Murphy as he slowly made his way up the stairs.

"Take your antibiotic!" Kate shouted after them while scrubbing the table fervently with both hands.

About twenty minutes later, Brad came back downstairs to find Kate aggressively cleaning the bathroom and muttering to herself.

"Hey," he said.

"What the hell was that?" was Kate's angry reply.

"You're obviously upset, why don't you put down the spray bottle and the scrub brush and we'll take a walk so I can explain," Brad was taking the bottle and brush from her as he said it. He took her by the arm, placed his hand on her lower back and moved her toward the door and outside. They started walking the trail toward the airstrip.

"Murphy is very embarrassed."

"He should be!"

Brad took a deep breath, "It's not his fault. Most of our safe houses offer what could be called 'comfort girls' for our men who have been, and will be, isolated for an extended period of time. It kind of helps, shall we say, keep them calm and ultimately on task."

Kate screwed up her face, "What?"

"I don't really wish to debate the merits of the practice," he could see the indignation on Kate's face. "Usually these individuals are separate from the safe house manager, but Murphy assumed given the location, your duty was to serve as both. Don't worry, I've set him straight. He meant no harm and I will make sure your role is clearly defined in the guest briefings in the future."

Kate was irritated by what she heard and strongly disapproved of using female agents as the equivalent of call girls to calm men down and manipulate them back into the field. Yet, it shed some light on one thing Brad may have been protecting her from when she considered joining the Agency. When it came to Murphy's behavior, she was beginning to empathize. He was as much a victim of the Agency culture as the women were. "I am choosing to make no further comments on this issue," Kate said harshly as she turned abruptly and headed back toward the cabin. Brad kept walking.

CHAPTER 9

The following morning Kate was in the kitchen pouring herself a bowl of Raisin Bran when Murphy apprehensively stepped in. "I…I want to sincerely apologize for what happened last night. I made assumptions I had no business making and frankly I'm quite ashamed of myself. I have the utmost respect for the work house managers do and I certainly never intended to offend you." His head was lowered and he was looking at Kate through the tops of his eyes.

"Apology accepted. Besides, I have decided to be angry with Mr. Oakley about the incident rather than you."

"Don't be too hard on him, he has a difficult job to do. He already seems to feel somewhat guilty about putting you in this job for some reason. I don't think he needs any piling on." Murphy shook his head, saddened by the thought.

Kate sighed. "Don't worry too much about Mr. Oakley. He'll survive." She changed the subject abruptly. "What would you like for breakfast? There's cereal, oatmeal, eggs, bacon, sausage, or you could make some pancakes."

"I'm not very hungry this morning, I think I'll just have some toast. Do we have any jam?" Murphy asked opening the refrigerator, "Oh good, strawberry, my favorite."

Kate moved to the table to eat her cereal. Brad still hadn't come downstairs. She had been worried enough this morning to check to see if his shoes were in the entry and look for other signs that he had returned from his walk into the woods. His shoes were there and his book was missing from the coffee table all good signs that he had not become part of the food chain overnight. She was angry enough that she wasn't going to give him the satisfaction of knowing she cared by knocking on his bedroom door to check on him. Instead, she headed outside to start planting her vegetables. No point in showering until after she played in the dirt.

It took Kate about thirty minutes to place all the pots of vegetable plants in the garden to arrange the layout. Just as she was starting to think about digging holes and planting them, Brad arrived with a coffee cup in hand.

"Good morning," he said with no sense of apprehension in his voice, yet he had bags under his eyes and his shoulders were sloped indicating that had not rested well. *I've never seen that before,* Kate thought to herself as she returned his good morning.

"I could use a distraction," Brad said, "Can I interest you in a ride out toward the mines?"

"I suppose the vegetables can wait. Do you want some breakfast first?"

"I just had some cereal, but maybe we could pack a lunch?" The tone of his voice reminded Kate of her nieces and nephews when they wanted her to do something they feared she would say no to.

"Okay. I assume you're not going in your shorts, so why don't you get dressed and I'll pack a lunch."

By the time Kate had packed a lunch for the two of them and secured it to the back of one of the ATVs, Brad had reemerged from the cabin carrying two helmets. He handed one to Kate. They rode back to the main gravel road and followed it out to where the gold mines were. Brad insisted on stopping to introduce themselves to several of the miners. During this time, Kate became proficient at what seemed to be the ceremonial greeting between miners and others who wandered onto their claims. The miner would approach, pulling back a shirt or jacket to expose their firearm, Kate would pull back hers exposing that she too was armed. The miner would nod and they would allow their clothing to fall back over their guns. *So we have an understanding then,* seemed to be the message.

"Mornin', what can I do for you?" the first miner asked as he stepped down from the cab of a huge dump truck and pulled back his flannel shirt to expose his gun.

"I'm Brad and this is my friend Kate, we've recently moved out here and thought we'd introduce ourselves."

"You have a mining claim?" the man asked as he squinted and spat on the ground. He didn't offer his name.

"Nope, we were just ready to become a little more independent in case the whole world goes to hell. It seems to be heading that way."

"You've got that right, brother," the miner seemed to relax, "That's why I've been holding back some gold, it'll be the only currency as soon as the government collapses."

"Since there's not that many year 'round residents out here, we thought it was best to get to know them. It never hurts to know who is and is not supposed to be around here, am I right?"

"You got that right," the man replied, "We have thieves and outlaws out here too, but we do a pretty good job of self-policing, if you know what I mean." Kate didn't know what he meant, but nodded as if she did. "Let me know if you need anything, we have to look out for each other out here, ya know."

And so it went over several mines as Brad exercised his gift of building camaraderie out of paranoia.

Brad and Kate stopped at the roadhouse that served the miners to meet the owners. Mike and Margaret Dunlap turned out to be a friendly couple in their early 70s who didn't appear to suffer the psychoses that many miners in the area seemed to operate under. The Dunlaps invited them in for coffee.

"None of the other people we've visited with have invited us in for coffee, we appreciate the hospitality," Kate said enjoying her first sip. "Do you live out here year 'round?"

"No," Margaret answered. "We're retired now, but we were once school teachers and mined and ran the roadhouse in the summer as a bit of a hobby. Now we go to Florida in the winter." That explained their exemplary social skills compared to the others they'd spoken to.

"There are some year 'round folks out here you need to look out for though," Mike added. "The Penecott Mine is owned by a man named Ralph Snider and he's not quite right in the head. People say he has gold fever, but I suspect it's schizophrenia combined with alcohol. If you ever need to go out to his place do so between ten and noon, that's when he's usually at his best."

"Good to know," Brad said, raising his eyebrows.

"It's probably a shorter list to tell you who's approachable," Margaret offered appearing to throw Mike a look that said *that's enough of that.* "There's a nice young couple, the Van Horns, operating a small claim about six miles farther in. They've been here about two years now and have an eight-month old little girl. They usually enjoy company in the evening and love when people bring them books, they're always looking for something to read. There's also Ed Faria at Hook Mine and Penelope Casey who runs her family's old claim with a couple of hired hands just north of Chester Creek. Do you know where that is?" Brad looked at Kate, she nodded.

"We do have some drifters to be wary of too," Mike chimed in, "There's a man in his early twenties who calls himself Billy living in an old trailer sitting near the abandoned Acre Mine site. He has told some people here that he's wanted for rape and murder in Utah and they believe him. Billy was working at Faria's place, but the other workers ran him off because he drinks and gets violent."

Margaret nodded her head in agreement before adding, "And there's a small group of men and women living in tents near the burnt out Cache Creek cabin. Someone said they thought two people in that group were wanted for kidnapping in Fairbanks. We don't know exactly what they're doing up there, but there have been whispers of animal sacrifices and other occult-type activities. They've come by here a few times to issue 'warnings' about the end being near and dark triumphing over light, that sort of thing. Frankly, they give me the creeps. The rest of the drifters seem to be relatively harmless, just people dropping out of society for a while or having an Alaskan adventure."

Brad and Kate finished their visit and the Dunlaps said they would let others know that they were around so everyone knew they belonged in the area. "Have we finished our social obligations?" Kate asked Brad as they mounted their ATVs.

"I believe so."

"Well then, it's time to get off-road and find a great place for lunch"

They backtracked down the dirt road and crossed back over the bridge. Kate turned her ATV around and stopped at the bank of the snowmelt-swollen creek. Slowly, she maneuvered her machine over the large rocks that led down to the water. Without hesitation, Kate added power and rode the bucking machine through the current and across the slippery boulders beneath it. Stopping in the middle of the creek would allow the swift current to flush her downstream, but she kept going and climbed the rocks on the other bank. Kate turned to watch as Brad made his way across the river, all the while yelling "Woo-Hoo!" and other expressions of masculine joy.

"Okay, now I'm having fun!" he said when he joined Kate on the far bank. Kate smiled and shook her head.

Kate led on the trail through the pine and birch forest heading toward the foothills of the Alaska Range. Eventually the forest turned to scrub brush and short alders where they could see the treeless meadows of the foothills ahead. Kate pulled over and turned off her machine. It was so quiet they could hear the gentle breeze blowing. "Last chance for a private potty break. Once we cross the tree line there will be nowhere to hide." She walked out into the alders and scrub brush to do as she suggested. Brad did the same.

They proceeded up the hill, out of the trees, and onto the low tundra vegetation that covered the higher elevations of the hills. There were a variety of grasses, moss, and low growing flowers primarily in white, and yellow. Kate decided one of the things she would do this winter was identify the vegetation. They crested the hill to a spectacular view and a sign telling them they could go no farther or they would encroach on Denali National Park. They were on one of the lower foothills with the taller ones surrounding them. The vantage point did not allow them a full view of Denali, but to their right, behind the tallest foothill, rose the peak of Denali. It seemed close enough to touch. "Will this do?" Kate asked with a grin.

"Indeed," Brad replied taking in the view.

They spread the blanket on the ground and set out their lunch. Kate noticed the area was covered in alpine blueberries, she would have to come back late in the summer to harvest some. "So why were we getting so chummy with the neighbors today?" Kate asked placing air quotes around 'neighbors', "I thought the theme of this mission was to be reclusive?"

"I wanted your presence to be natural and not an anomaly. I also thought if they knew who we were, and believed we had similar values, they would be protective rather than suspicious. There's a small army of heavily armed people out here, I want them on your side."

Kate shrugged, unconvinced that it would make any difference in a place where people are most likely to keep to themselves and privacy is valued.

"I have a sudden urge to yodel or sing something about the hills being alive with music or something when I'm up here," Brad said, changing the subject.

"Wrong mountains. Here we recite the poetry of Robert Service. *The Cremation of Sam McGee* is always a crowd pleaser," Kate replied with a grin as she began to recite.

There are strange things done in the midnight sun
By the men who moil for gold;
The Arctic trails have their secret tales
That would make your blood run cold…

"I think too much of that might assault my happy, mellow mood and those feelings are much too rare lately," Brad said closing his eyes and taking a deep breath of the mountainous air and running his hand across the tundra vegetation. He turned to Kate, "There is nowhere else in the world I want to be right now than in this spot with present company and a PB&J on wheat."

"Me too." They smiled and Brad rubbed the top of Kate's hand gently.

They finished their lunch and took a photo inventory of the vegetation on Kate's phone so she could identify the plants later. After about an hour and a half they reluctantly returned to their ATVs and descended back to the cabin.

When they arrived, they found Murphy building a fire in the fire pit. He waved, "You're just in time! I found some lawn chairs in the shed and decided to start a fire we could sit around. I've been spending way too much time in front of that TV and decided some fresh air would do us all some good. Besides, I'm in the mood for hot dogs and s'mores." His enthusiasm was contagious. And that's how they spent the rest of their day.

Chapter 10

The next morning Kate went to the garden to once again try to plant her vegetables. She had the first row in the ground when Brad came out and pulled one of the lawn chairs next to the garden. He walked into the shed and came out with a large soaker-style water gun. He went to the spigot on the side of the cabin to fill the reservoir. Kate watched him quizzically as she planted. He sat in the chair and said, "It looks like you're making some progress today."

"I am," Kate said with a chuckle, "and how are you this morning?"

"I have to leave and return to reality and I don't really want to go."

"Hey, watch what you're calling reality. This *is* my reality."

"You're one lucky woman. I wonder if the CIA would give me a sabbatical?"

Brad leaned back in the chair and while Kate planted, he began taking aim at objects with the water gun testing himself for both accuracy and distance. Kate shook her head and muttered something to herself about guns being an extension of the male anatomy. He put the gun in his lap and asked, "So what is the status of Max's software company? Do you plan to sell, or operate it?"

"Well, my current plan is to continue to operate it. Max hired a competent staff and I've offered his right hand man a significant share of profits and annual growth to serve as general manger. He's a sharp guy and I have a great deal of confidence in him. I don't know how this arrangement will work out long term, as he may eventually decide to start his own company, but for now it provides a good, relatively passive income stream for me, and continuity for our client base. I meet with them once a month as kind of a one-person Board of Directors to keep a handle on things."

Kate suspected Brad already knew this as allowing the monthly report from her accountant to be brought in with the supplies as well as facilitating a secure monthly call with company management were two of her conditions for taking the assignment.

"Do you know what projects Max was working on personally before he disappeared?" Brad asked.

"I've covered all this with the FBI, but if you must know, on the programming side he was working closely with staff on a proprietary management information and logistics system that could be used by the oil and gas industry. It was the first time they tried to develop an off-the-shelf software product that could be sold industry-wide rather than creating unique systems for individual clients. Max believed it would make communication and integration across companies, suppliers, and clients much easier."

"Was the company consulting on any outside projects?"

"Yes, and he generally popped-in on most large projects just to see how things were going. There were two consulting projects he was checking in on regularly and one he was actively involved in just before his disappearance. The first was an educational business simulation that was a joint project with Harvard and the second was a smaller project with a cargo airline to develop the systems for a sales incentive program.

The project he ended up actively participating in involved improving the order/trader matching system at a large Wall Street firm called Lasarlume. It was a system that was part internal audit, part management information, and part payroll. It was designed to link traders to the trades they made more effectively and efficiently."

"Aren't traders and trades linked automatically when the orders are entered."

" Yes and no. Linking orders to traders may sound like an easy thing to do, but somehow as trades moved around the market and executed trades were reported, occasionally the identity of the trader gets dropped. This has been a problem for years at most companies on Wall Street. Lasarlume asked Max's company to consult on both internal and system-wide improvements to prevent it from happening. While they were successful in reducing the number of 'orphan orders', there remained an unacceptably large number of orders that were not matched to traders and in some cases, were even missing information on the trading firm. Max was actively working with the team to try to find a solution."

"What did he think the problem was?"

"I don't know."

"Are you sure?" Brad asked as he squirted Kate on the side of the head with the water gun.

"Hey!" Kate yelled wiping at the water in her hair and glaring at Brad.

"Did he think the problems were internal to the companies or external?"

"He didn't say," Kate said with added volume in her voice. *Squirt.* Brad hit her in the forehead.

"Stop it!"

"Did he ever express any concerns that he was poking around where someone didn't want him?"

"No! We never really talked about it in detail!" *Squirt.* A precise shot to the center of her chest.

"What the hell is the matter with you?! Why don't you just take me into the shed and waterboard me, it might be quicker and it would definitely be less irritating."

"We don't do that anymore" *Squirt.* Forehead again.

Kate stood, stomped her foot and yelled, "What is it you're looking for? I don't know anything. If I could help don't you think I would? What is it you want me to say?"

Brad set the water gun on the ground. "Calm down," he said pushing the palms of his hands in Kate's direction. "Okay, so you don't know the technical details, but how did he seem? What was his mood?"

"Max seemed like himself except he expressed frustration when talking about the project. He couldn't figure out what the problem was or why it had only emerged in the past three years or so. There had been similar problems in the European Union several years before, but they had stopped so there were no clues to be gained there."

"Did he contact anyone for help?"

"I know he had made some calls to regulators and firms in the EU before he left for Asia to see if they had any ideas, but they didn't. He also asked me, but all I could do was give him a history of the EU's problem. I didn't have any good answers either."

"Hmmm," Brad said walking over to Kate while removing his handkerchief from the front pocket of his jeans. When he reached her, he took her chin in his hand and started patting her face dry with his handkerchief. "Sorry, but I couldn't help myself." He smiled; Kate scowled. "I shouldn't have teased you," Brad said before kissing her on the forehead and returning to the cabin. Kate went back to her vegetables, digging furiously and therapeutically.

Since Brad was leaving at 1:00, they each made themselves a sandwich and gathered at the table for lunch.

"So you're getting sprung today, huh?" Murphy said to Brad.

"I am, but unlike you, I will have to keep coming back occasionally. Once you're sprung, we hope you're out for good." They both smiled and Murphy nodded his head vigorously.

Brad's bag was in the arctic entry near the door. After lunch the two men stayed at the table, swapped war stories and talked about the batting averages of a long list of famous and obscure baseball players. They had a deep bench.

Kate showered and then went out to hook the trailer to the ATV. Brad and Murphy came out, shook hands like two people who have enjoyed each other's company, but would probably never see each other again. It struck Kate that the lack of male companionship might be hard on Murphy. He was a guy's guy. Brad threw his bag in the trailer and climbed aboard the ATV with Kate.

The pair arrived at the airstrip shortly before the plane arrived. When it landed, the same pilot hopped out and Kate suspected he might be their regular. "Afternoon, Ma'am," he said with a wave.

Brad and the pilot loaded the supplies he had brought into the ATV trailer and Brad threw his bag into the small cargo area of the plane. The pilot saluted Kate and headed for the plane to do his walk around. He held up two fingers in Brad's direction, "Two minutes," he instructed.

Brad walked over to Kate and took both of her hands in his. "Thanks for putting up with me," he said looking at the ground.

"It was my pleasure."

"Per our agreement I have a couple of things for you," Brad said dropping her hands and reaching into his shirt pocket. He pulled out a key on a chain and put it around Kate's neck. "This is the key to the locked box that was brought in when Murphy arrived. It's in the communications room and contains Max's things." Kate swallowed hard and nodded. He pulled out a thumb drive and placed it in the front pocket of her jeans. "This is the European stock market data you requested for your research. Please keep it locked up when you're not using it." Kate placed her hand over her pocket as if to secure the contents while Brad turned and walked toward the plane. "Oh, and Kate," he said turning, "I want you to know that I'm aware Max's death has been difficult for you, so I've been trying to give you some time and space. But at some point, I'm going to want to kiss you again."

Kate nodded almost imperceptibly and bit her lower lip. Brad boarded the airplane and waved as they started down the runway.

CHAPTER 11

Not long after Brad's departure, Murphy started to feel quite a bit better and took over mowing the airstrip and creating a system to better organize supplies. He had a knack for organization that made Kate wish she could turn him loose on her closets for about a week. They also started collaborating on menus a week in advance so they could more accurately order supplies and Murphy took over half the cooking duties. Kate also thought it would be a good idea to cook some soups, stews, and pies to put in the freezer for when new guests arrived that they hadn't planned for. Murphy agreed and offered to make some of his grandmother's chocolate chip cookie dough for the freezer in case emergency cravings arose. It was good to be prepared.

Every night after dinner, Kate and Murphy had started to play dominos or cribbage. Murphy was very competitive, whereas, Kate didn't feel the need for such competitive stress in her recreational activities. This generally meant that Kate was a much better loser than Murphy, who seemed to take it personally. His inability to accept defeat led to demands for rematches, which fostered their evening game ritual.

They also found themselves leaving the radio on most of the time instead of just during the message portion Kate was required to listen to. It gave the two of them a link to civilization and a passive sense of being part of a community. Over time through the radio classified ads, messages, and community comment type call-in shows they felt like they were getting to know some of the locals, at least superficially. "Oh boy, Joan isn't going to like Ted's comment!"

Murphy would say as they listened to a community comment program and sure enough, three calls later Joan's voice would come on the air berating Ted.

At times Kate felt like a voyeur, only slightly better than a peeping tom. Although Hollywood had created an entire industry based on the entertainment value of other people's reality, she sometimes felt uncomfortable hiding people within a community she watched, but didn't participate in. The realities Kate and her guests were living were far from here, connected to this one only by the vaporous trail of an airplane. It felt like they were an entire dimension removed from the people they heard on the radio.

On the Saturday following Brad's extraction from their covert point in the middle of the vast Alaskan wilderness, Kate received a message during dinner informing her she would be receiving two guests the following morning. "Would you like a roommate Murph?" Kate asked as they ate their apple crisp, "Or should I have them bunk together?"

"I don't mind a roommate, but let's see who they are and how they're doing before we decide on room assignments. Some people want to be alone when they come in, other's need the security of knowing someone else is there to watch their back so they can rest."

"I hadn't considered that Murph, but I will in the future. Thanks for the advice. I'll get better at this."

"You're doing great," Murphy offered as encouragement before taking another bite of his desert.

In the morning both Kate and Murphy boarded ATVs and headed for the airstrip, Murphy pulling the trailer. "Good morning ma'am," the usual pilot said, tipping his ball cap at Kate.

"Good morning!"

"Since your population is doubling I brought along some extra milk, juice, and eggs to get you by until the next supply run."

"Good thinking!" Kate said, still not used to the fact that she couldn't drive to the store if she ran out.

The pilot handed Murphy an envelope, "Looks like you have orders son, I'll be taking you out on the supply run in four days." Murphy looked at the orders with a mix of delight and trepidation.

"Thanks," he said with a hint of excitement.

The two new guests deplaned, introductions were made, and the trailer loaded. The short-term guest, Robert, was a man not unlike Murphy in personality or physical description and the two of them hit it off immediately. The long-term guest, Joe, was quite different. He appeared to be in his late 30s to early 40s, about six feet tall and slender with sandy blonde hair cut short, round wire-rimmed glasses, a long nose, and an aura that implied an intelligent and pensive, yet friendly, nature. His mannerisms appeared deliberate as if they had to be planned moments before execution. He looked like an accountant and Kate couldn't figure out what possible 'excitement' this man could have experienced that would put him in need of a long-term stay at a safe house. Although, she supposed it was that very characteristic that made him an effective at his job, assuming he was effective and not here because he screwed something up.

Kate learned over time that tough-looking agents like Murphy and Robert tended to be the exception whereas Joe was more the rule when it came to CIA employees. Apparently the CIA was full of people who resembled accountants and she would forever blame the Agency's scandals and shortcomings on this lack of diversity. Sometimes you need some muscle because a balance sheet just won't do.

Murphy confirmed Kate's airstrip deduction about which man would be his roommate as the quartet arrived at the cabin, "Robert, why don't you bunk with me and we'll give Joe a room to himself. That work for you Joe?"

"Absolutely," Joe said, grabbing his bags as the others did the same.

"Come on, I'll show you around," Murphy offered grabbing some of the extra supplies the pilot brought, while Kate carried the rest. The three men bounded in ahead of her and Murphy had them depositing outerwear and shoes in the lockers in the arctic entryway when she arrived.

Kate had put a beef roast in the slow cooker for dinner and the cabin smelled great when they walked in. The momentary closed eyes and upturned noses on the men indicated they noticed, though no one said anything. The radio was on and as they passed Murphy started briefing them about the cast of local characters. He looked like a camp councilor orienting the new campers. *I'll miss his enthusiasm, but not his volume level*, she thought.

After showing the men their rooms and dropping their bags, Murphy brought them downstairs. "They're hungry, I'm gonna show 'em where things are so they can fix a sammich." Murphy said jerking his thumb toward the kitchen.

"Very well," Kate said, "I'll be in the garden pulling weeds."

A few minutes later Joe emerged from the cabin, sandwich in hand, and stood on the steps inhaling deeply. "This air is fantastic. Is this what it's supposed to smell like? I've forgotten."

"I believe it is," Kate replied, "Pull up a chair if you'd like and eat your sandwich in the air as God intended." He did.

"I'm sorry if I'm disturbing you, but Robert is discussing the complexities of his extraction from wherever he was with a level of vehemence I'm not quite ready for yet. The cabin is small, how do you stand the din?"

"Well, this is the first time I've had two loud, fervent people here, so perhaps we will find out. I find gardening helps most things," Kate offered a smile.

"Indeed. My mother used to have an incredible rose garden at the house where I grew up and I have very fond memories of helping her prune and harvest roses. It centers you somehow; connects you to the earth, very pleasant."

"I do some of my deepest thinking in the garden. I'm going to have to come up with a way to have deep thoughts during the winter months though. Maybe I need to get one of those little boxes with the sand and the tiny rake…a Zen garden I believe they call it."

"Somehow I think that wouldn't be the same," Joe chuckled to himself. "So, we were told to leave you alone so you could work, is gardening your work or is there something else?"

"No, the garden is relaxation. I have some research projects I need to work on."

"How are they going?"

"Well, to be honest, I haven't started them quite yet."

"Why not? This seems like the perfect place to get some work done."

"Let's just say I haven't been in the mood yet. It's complicated"

"I understand things can be complicated. Let me know if there's anything I can do that will help get you in the mood…sorry…that sounded bad…but I hope you know what I mean."

"I do," Kate giggled lightly, "and I appreciate your support Joe."

"Good. In the meantime, I'm going to go have a gentle discussion with our housemates about the difference between inside and outside voices," Joe said as he stood while dramatically popping the last bite of turkey sandwich into his mouth and brushing his hands together to discharge any crumbs. Kate decided having an accountant-type around might be all right.

That evening the routine changed. Murphy and Robert played poker in the great room, while Kate and Joe played cribbage at the dining table. Joe preferred chess, but Kate didn't play. When the poker players became too loud, Joe would issue a stern, "Gentleman!" and they would apologize and simmer down. "You said you were planning to identify the plants you found in the foothills," Joe said. Kate had mentioned it over dinner. "I'd love to help you with that. Would you be willing to print the pictures so I can take a look at them? It would give me something to do while I'm here at least."

"Of course," Kate said, "I'll print them before I go to bed."

The next morning Kate enjoyed some much-needed serenity with a cup of coffee and the panoramic view of the Alaska Range. There were wispy clouds slowly moving in front of Denali, just below the peak. Kate suspected the top third of the mountain would be encased in clouds by afternoon. After 20 minutes, all three men tromped down the stairs to start their day. *Serenity must be lost to be found,* Kate thought. They greeted her simultaneously.

"Joe tells us you haven't been working," Murphy said as Kate slid Joe a sideways glance, "We're going to give you some time alone this morning so you can. The leg's feeling better so Robert and I are gonna go for a run and throw some logs around and stuff to get some exercise after breakfast."

"Really," Kate said dryly looking Joe straight in the face this time, "Well, if you're going to go for a run you might want to take my gun, you don't want to run into anything that thinks *you're* breakfast."

"Not to worry, we brought our own," Robert chimed in.

"*I'll* be reading a book," Joe said smugly.

After breakfast Murphy and Robert stretched and went for a run saying they should be back on the property to finish their workout within forty-five minutes. After they left, Kate confronted Joe, "Pardon me?" she said with irritation.

"Don't be angry, last night I started to think about how I could help you get...well...in the mood, as you put it, and decided some quiet time would be a good place to start. While I don't know what complications you arrived with, I can help minimize the complications here. I promise, I won't do it again if you will go upstairs and work for an hour. I don't care if all you do is stare at the computer, you just need to take the first step and maybe start a routine."

He's right, Kate thought and rubbed her face with both hands. "All right," she said, "one hour."

"Great, I'll do the dishes."

Kate unlocked the communication room door and sat down on the wheeled stool that served as a desk chair. She tried to adjust the height of the stool, but found it difficult. Eventually, she managed to lower it to a better position, but made a mental note to lubricate it. "Where to start?" she asked with a heavy sigh. Kate knew she wasn't ready to start going through Max's things, so she popped the thumb drive Brad had given her into the laptop. She clicked on the external drive icon and then the single file that resided within it.

Data for a six-month period from major EU markets appeared on the screen. As part of her research on market security, Kate was planning to explore a series of mini crashes in European markets to try to find the causes. In a *market* crash, the value of the entire financial market drops suddenly and steeply before recovering nearly as quickly, a *mini* crash is when the same thing happens to a single stock.

The EU had experienced several years of daily sporadic mini crashes of individual stocks that no one fully understood. Many theories had been proposed and pundits had whipped the public and legislators into a frenzy, asserting markets were no longer reliable or fair. "People are cheating," one prominent pundit proclaimed, "They are manipulating the market for their own gain by tricking people into selling so they can buy when the price drops suddenly and then sell again when the price goes up."

Speculation about how this alleged cheating was being done sparked investigations of brokerage firms and exchanges. These investigations ultimately forced several firms out of business as customers fled to other institutions as rumors spread quickly that customer's assets might be frozen. Other firms began fleeing EU countries for the United States and Japan as well as emerging financial markets like Russia, Brazil, Singapore, China, and even Mexico as regulations designed to curb the alleged cheating became too difficult to comply with and made the EU financial markets less efficient. The European financial system was now in an all-encompassing crisis and it all started with several years of mini crashes. The mini crashes in Europe had since stopped, making regulators reluctant to ease market restrictions for fear they would return. The reality was that so many new policies had been put into place within such a short period of time, that there was no way to know which, if any, had curbed the mini crashes.

From a risk management perspective, Kate knew that understanding the root causes of the mini crashes was important to protect markets from fear-induced interference that could cause more harm than good as it had in the Europe Union. This problem had become especially urgent, as mini crashes had occurred several times in the U. S. markets over the past few months. While their existence was not widely known to the general public, insiders were concerned and looking for answers.

Kate started her analysis by looking for stocks that had sudden price drops that were greater than two standard deviations from the average price changes during any day within the month. She wrote a simple algorithm and ran it against the data. A list of twenty-three stocks emerged. All twenty-three were large-cap stocks—stocks that had a market value of greater than 10 billion U.S. dollars when you multiplied the number of the company's shares of stock outstanding by its stock price per share. Large-cap stocks are generally traded more frequently than mid- or small-cap stocks. Kate didn't know if their size was significant, but she made a note of it.

Kate created one spreadsheet for each of the twenty-three stocks that contained the stock's daily closing price data. On days when there were mini crashes, she added the time of the crash as well as the pre-crash price, the low price, and the price at the peak of the price recovery. She then started to make a list of all the factors that might cause the price of a stock to drop: Bad news about the company (an employee, lawsuit, licensing or product problem, surprises in a quarterly or annual report, etc.), sale of a large block of stock by a single or multiple stockholders, competitor news, discontinuing a stock buy-back program, overall market decline, macroeconomic factors, hardware or software problems, trader error, and new regulations. There were about twenty factors Kate came up with off the top of her head and there would probably be more over time. Researching the issues to see if any of them were in place and contributed to the mini crashes was going to take a long time. Good thing she had a long winter ahead of her. Kate started her research by searching the Internet for news about the companies around the time of the crashes.

Kate started to feel like she needed a snack and was surprised when her watch read 11:30am. *Wow*, she thought rubbing her eyes, *that time went fast*. She made her way down the stairs to find Joe seated on the couch with pictures and books spread out in front of him on the coffee table. "Hi," he said, "Looks like you got some work done."

"I have a good foundation," Kate said, "but I've barely scratched the surface."

"Well, I'm proud of you. Come see what I've been working on." He motioned for Kate to come over. Kate noticed the pictures on the table were the ones she'd taken in the foothills. Joe had attached small adhesive labels to some of them in the lower right hand corner. He waived his hand over the pictures. "There were a couple of books on the shelf on Alaskan flora and fauna and I've made some good progress identifying the plants. I've labeled the ones I'm certain of, but I still have a couple that are giving me fits." Kate sat next to him and they spent what was left of the morning going through the photos. He had not only learned the names of the plants, but also information about their histories, edibility, and medicinal uses, which he had written on the back.

Chapter 12

Murphy had been gone from the safe house for about three weeks and Kate, Robert, and Joe had settled into their own routine. Kate spent her mornings in the communication room looking for correlations between events and the mini crashes of individual stocks and spent part of her afternoons working in the garden. The rest of her days were spent taking care of chores like ordering supplies, cleaning the solar panel, starting the pump generator to refill the water pressure tank, changing water filters, and her share of the cooking duties. Joe was teaching Robert how to play chess and the men took turns cutting the grass at the airstrip, chopping wood, meeting the supply flights, and sharing the other basic maintenance needs of the cabin. Robert usually took a daily run, while Joe enjoyed helping Kate in the garden. Kate enjoyed Joe's companionship; he was smart, pleasant, and easy to talk to.

Today Kate and Joe decided the raspberry patch needed weeding, which required donning gloves and long sleeves to avoid tearing up their arms with thorns. "As far as safe houses go, this one is much more pleasant than most," Joe remarked as he pulled back some of the thorny bushes so Kate could reach in and pull out the weeds. "Most safe houses are in much more populated areas and require guests to stay indoors with all the shades drawn in order to avoid being seen. Here we can go outside, a rare treat for those in hiding."

"I can't imagine being cooped up inside all day. I need to get out and breathe some fresh air every day", Kate said while taking a deep breath.

"This is a great assignment, you're lucky," Joe said matter-of-factly.

"Let's wait until winter sets in before you jump to any conclusions about the ideal nature of this assignment," Kate said. Joe smiled and nodded his head in agreement.

"If it's none of my business Kate you can tell me, but how are you doing? They told me before I got here that you had recently lost your husband and I notice you seem to already be somewhat less withdrawn than when I arrived. When I got here, you seemed to be…I don't know…spending a lot of time inside your own head or you were depressed or something. That's not a criticism, just an observation, but you seem to be doing better."

It struck Kate as odd that Joe had been briefed about her husband's passing. She shrugged it off. "Well, I still have some things hanging over my head regarding his death, but work and having people around helps."

"Tell me about him."

"I'll just say this, he was a good man, funny, smart, sensitive, a good listener, and we loved each other very much. It's funny, I thought the things I would miss most about him would be his sense of humor, his companionship, and his ability to cheer me up when I was feeling down, but what I miss most is intimacy. I find myself starting to miss making love to him and then laying in his arms afterward and talking about the most mundane things like what color to paint the bathroom or where we should go for dinner Friday night. I didn't expect that."

"That's a good sign though, isn't it? I would think an awakening of one's desire for intimacy is a sign of healing. When I think about the worst breakup I ever had with a woman, I swore I would never get close to someone ever again. It took a while, but eventually I met someone and that yearning for intimacy came back. In your case, since you experienced your loss through death rather than a breakup, it makes sense that your desire for intimacy would be directed toward your late husband, but it might be a sign that you've started to move beyond your desire to isolate and your feelings of anger and depression, and are heading toward a healthy acceptance of what has happened."

"Perhaps," Kate said staring out toward some distant point in contemplation.

Joe changed the subject to a discussion about when the raspberries might be ready. Kate said they should start to see some ripen by mid-August.

The trio's routine continued until the second week in August, when word came that a new guest and a support person would be driving in. Kate was to meet them at the Amber Creek parking lot for transport via ATVs. With the terrible condition the roads were in past that point, it made a lot of sense to leave the vehicle behind and ride the last six miles or so on ATVs. In the winter, the Amber Creek parking lot was as far as the road into the area was plowed. After that point you had to travel by snow machine to get to the more remote parts of Trapper Creek where they were. Once it started to snow, Kate would have to drive her truck out and park it in the lot for the winter in case they needed to get out of the area for any reason. Kate didn't know what they meant when they said a 'support person' would be coming, but she assumed it would most likely be a military or Agency person. Joe offered to drive the second ATV and Kate towed the trailer.

As they approached the parking lot, Kate could see Brad leaning with his back against the bed of a pickup truck. He must be the support person they promised. Kate smiled and waved as Brad pulled himself up off the truck and grabbed two duffels out of the bed. When they arrived Kate and Joe removed their helmets and dismounted the ATVs as Brad dropped the duffels into the trailer. Kate felt like she'd been on a horse too long and bent over and touched her toes to loosen up her back and hips. As she rolled back up to a standing position, Brad was opening the passenger side door of the truck and trying to coax a man out of the seat. The man who finally emerged was relatively short, about five foot six, balding, and while not exactly fat, he would be described as 'pleasingly plump' by Kate's 6th grade teacher who seemed to identify that trait in people with some regularity. The noises he was making, however, were less than pleasant and definitely those of someone who was unhappy about his current situation.

"I can't believe you've taken me to this God forsaken place. These bugs are insufferable!" the man said while swatting at his head in a way that was certain to entertain the bugs, but was grossly ineffective at discouraging them. He sneezed three times and wiped his nose with a fast food napkin. His eyes looked glassy and his cheeks were red.

"I told you to put on bug repellent. It's the only way to keep them at bay," Brad was obviously irritated with the man.

"But my asthma! Why don't you just take me somewhere else? Surly I can hide out at a 5-star hotel with room service somewhere?" More sneezing. More blowing.

"Hi, I'm Kate," she held out her hand.

"Charmed I'm sure," the man said ignoring her hand and brushing past her to get closer to the ATVs.

"You certainly don't expect me to ride on one of these, do you?!" he looked at Brad while pointing at the ATV.

"Kate, this is *Mr.* Delgado," Brad said emphasizing the 'Mr' as if he had been reminded repeatedly to use it. "And yes, I do expect you to ride on one of those, unless *Mr.* Delgado prefers to ride in the trailer with the luggage."

"How dare you!" Mr. Delgado said harshly, still swatting like a man possessed.

"The good news, Mr. Delgado, is that once we get moving, the bugs will leave you alone," Kate tossed out as an incentive while offering him a helmet.

"I doubt it, bugs love me!" Mr. Delgado grabbed the helmet abruptly, walked toward Kate's ATV, and got on.

As Brad walked past, he whispered in Kate's ear, "Bugs love him because he's rotten." Kate smirked.

The entire way to the cabin Delgado howled about his back hurting as he clutched at Kate's shirt and arms exclaiming she was driving too fast and that he was going to die in this terrible place. Kate tried to ignore him and concentrate on her driving for fear her growing impulse to leave him on the side of the trail would become too overwhelming to suppress. She fantasized that Joe and Brad had chosen to follow behind her ATV so they could run Delgado over if she kicked him off. After all, Brad had already spent more than two and a half hours with the man.

When they arrived at the cabin, Delgado quickly removed himself from the ATV and sat on the steps with his face in his hands. He was wheezing and coughing. "I feel terrible," he said.

"Mr. Delgado is ill," Brad said to Kate, "The doctor has checked him out and says its just a virus and with rest and fluids he should feel better within the next 7 to 10 days."

"Great," Kate said sarcastically.

"Let's go inside Mr. Delgado and get you a glass of juice," Joe said taking him by the arm to help him up.

When they entered the cabin, Delgado went into a fit of coughing and sneezing. Robert came over and handed him a box of tissues. "Bless you and welcome," he said to Delgado. Delgado managed only to groan as he made his way to the dining table to sit down and manage his mucus.

"This is Mr. Delgado," Kate offered as introduction.

"Nice to meet you Delgado," Robert said as he relieved Brad of the bags.

Delgado stood up with some effort and his face turned a darker shade of crimson. He moved close to Robert and leaned into him, "That's *Mr.* Delgado. I am a man with great responsibility in charge of many people and I will be treated with the respect I deserve!" His voice cracked with rage and virus.

Robert stepped backwards as Brad yelled, "Hey!", Joe "Wait a minute!", and Kate "That's enough!" in a shriek that made all four men stop and look at her.

"Listen Delgado, I don't care who you are outside this cabin, but here all guests are equal and there is only one person in charge and that person is me! I would suggest that you go upstairs, unpack your things, take a shower if you'd like, and be down here in an hour and a half for dinner with a new attitude!" Delgado opened his mouth to speak, but after looking around the room, quickly closed it.

"Why don't you bunk with me Delgado," Joe said taking his bag from Robert and giving Delgado a gentle push toward the stairs. "Tonight is Dr. Kate's night to cook and I'm sure you don't want to miss one of her dinners." Kate suspected he added the "Dr." to Kate's name while dropping the "Mr." from Delgado's to emphasize the chain of command.

Kate was shaking and, as Delgado went up the stairs, she stomped out of the cabin and walked several laps around it. She forced herself to start thinking about dinner as a way to redirect her mind as she took deep breaths and shook her hands as if she had just touched something hot. She walked to the power house and started the well pump generator. She didn't know if the water tank needed to be filled, but it gave her something to do. While she was there, she opened the freezer and took out a large container of frozen chicken noodle soup and a smaller one of crab cakes. She remained outside until the well pump stopped, indicating the tank was full, and then turned off the generator.

When Kate re-entered the cabin, Robert was watching television and the others were nowhere in sight. Kate turned knobs to preheat the oven and placed a large pot on the stove. She ran some hot water over the container of soup to loosen it and then dropped the frozen mass into the pot, turning on a low flame under it. Crab cakes were arranged on a cookie sheet and when the oven was ready, she turned it down and inserted the pan. In the refrigerator she found some bib lettuce, kale, and spinach, which she shredded and placed in a large mixing bowl. Olive oil, balsamic vinegar, and minced garlic were whisked together in a small bowl, poured over the greens, and tossed together. Kate divided the salad onto the side of five plates and topped it with feta cheese, sunflower seeds, grape tomatoes, and miniature yellow peppers.

Joe, Robert, and Delgado could be heard speaking quietly in the great room. She couldn't hear the conversation and that was okay with her. At the appointed dinnertime, Joe poked his head into the kitchen and asked how long before they should get themselves to the table. "If you will take drink orders and set the beverages out, dinner will be ready by the time you're done." Joe saluted and went out to see what everyone wanted to drink. Kate pulled the crab cakes out of the oven and used a spatula to place two on each plate next to the salad and ladled soup into small, cup-sized bowls that she also added to the plates.

The three men were seated at the table when she arrived with the food. "I thought some chicken soup might be good for the health of our new guest.

Does anyone know if Oakley will be joining us?" Kate asked, careful not to precede it with "Mr."

"Haven't seen him," Joe replied.

Kate walked up the stairs and as she approached the communications room noticed a paperclip sticking out of the lock on the door. The paperclip indicated that Brad was in the room working on something confidential; she wouldn't knock. Instead, she returned to the kitchen and placed his plate in the refrigerator so he could eat later.

As they ate, Kate said, "Joe, since Delgado is sick, it might be better if you gave him the room to himself and bunked with Robert for a few days. We can put Oakley on the sofa sleeper."

"We've already thought of that," Robert said, "It was Delgado's idea actually, he was afraid he'd keep Joe up with his coughing and sneezing and doesn't want to make him sick."

"An excellent idea, Delgado," Kate said.

"T'anks," Delgado said no longer able to manage the 'th' sound through the congestion. There was no fight left in him. He seemed to be getting worse.

They finished dinner and applesauce cake for dessert with no appearance by Brad. It was Joe's turn to do the dishes, but Kate told him she'd do them so she could have a little time to herself. She was feeling stressed, trapped, and was seeking refuge in the kitchen before the entire cabin closed in on her. It wasn't even winter yet.

As Kate was starting to put the food away, she remembered something. From the cabinet she pulled out a mug and filled the kettle with water and placed it on the stove. When the water boiled, she poured it over a peppermint teabag in the mug, added honey and lemon, and carried the cup of tea to her room. Guests were allowed to have beer and wine, but were limited to two drinks a day, however, Kate had snuck in a bottle of bourbon and peppermint schnapps, which she kept hidden in her room for just such an occasion. She poured a shot of the bourbon into the tea.

Delgado was having a coughing fit when Kate knocked on his door. "Come in," he said weakly between gasps.

"Hi, I'm sorry you're feeling poorly, but I have something that might help," Kate sat on the edge of the bed, "I can offer you a hot toddy as long as you do me a favor and don't tell anyone I have bourbon in this cabin."

"Bourbon, what bourbon," Delgado said sitting up and taking the mug from Kate. He breathed in the steam emitting from the mug, "You're an angel."

"I'll leave you to it then. Try to get some rest. As they say, this too shall pass." As Kate walked toward the stairs, she noticed Joe and Robert must have been in their room. Based on the sounds coming through the door, she guessed Robert had convinced Joe to play poker. It appeared Joe was providing Kate with some space at great personal expense; he hated poker. She would need to do something nice for him. He was a good man.

The weight of the dishwasher detergent container indicated it should be added to the supply list or they'd be roughing it and washing dishes by hand before long. Surly that would upset Delgado's asthma in some way. Brad walked into the kitchen emitting a low, breathy sigh. He placed his hands on the edge of the counter to brace himself, lowered his head and stretched. He turned toward Kate, "I've had a very bad day."

"Anything you would like to talk about."

"Yes, but I can't." He looked defeated and vulnerable, a look Kate had never seen on Brad, and he wore it awkwardly. "Our new friend Delgado was the least of my problems today, if you can believe that." He shook his head "What is that guy's problem?"

"I don't know, but it was very charitable of Robert to offer him a box of tissues when we walked in, I was ready to let him drown in his own mucus at that point," they laughed and then, without warning, Kate started to cry.

"Whoa, whoa, whoa, what's the matter?"

"All I want to do right now is get in my truck and go home," she said between sobs while trying to catch her breath, "I'm sick of all of it, the guests, my research, everything."

Brad hugged her tightly, "But who'd take care of the garden?"

"Yeah," Kate said with a snort and more tears.

"It'll be okay, I promise," Brad said stroking her hair, "So what's wrong with your research?"

"I haven't been able to find any correlations yet between the mini crashes and potential precipitating events, but instead have come across reports of another problem that is equally as puzzling. Some brokers are claiming that when they enter their buy or sell trade orders, before they even hit the enter key to submit them, the price of the stock starts to rapidly move up and down by a few cents. It makes no sense because there is no way to know an order is being entered and demand for the stock is changing before it's submitted. Now I have two problems I can't figure out. It's very frustrating."

"You'll figure it out, you just haven't looked under the right rock yet. Hang in there." Brad rubbed her back and kissed her warmly on the cheek. When he did, Kate could smell his aftershave, feel his growing warmth, and the roughness of the whiskers he hadn't shaved in at least 24 hours. It hit her. It started with an ache in her belly that spread to the rest of her body like an electric current. Brad felt it too. They were both vulnerable and they needed each other for strength. Brad relaxed his embrace enough to see her face.

"I want to kiss you," he said.

"Yes," Kate said with a single nod.

He pressed his lips against hers. Their kissing escalated easily as their familiarity with each other resurfaced. "Will you let me make love to you?" Brad asked with a look that implored her.

A whispered "Yes," was all Kate could manage as she felt like all the air had been taken out of the room. They made their way to her bedroom.

An hour later they lay silently in each other's arms trying to catch their breath and basking in the momentary feeling of well being orgasm provides. The sex had been charged with the urgency and intensity that feeling alone fuels. "Wow, I think you might have made me blush." Brad whispered hoarsely before rolling over to kiss Kate, "I haven't been intimate with anyone in more than four years, but you've flipped a switch that may make me insatiable. I hope that wasn't our last time."

"You're lying," Kate said picking her head slightly off the pillow, "There is no way you've been celibate for more than four years."

"Unfortunately, it's true."

"But why? I'm sure you've had opportunities."

"Yes, but no one felt right. I've found it increasingly difficult to trust women enough to be intimate. I'm starting to imagine foreign female spies everywhere who want to harvest information from me, or fear becoming emotionally involved will make me vulnerable in some way. I've watched way too many men betray their countries to protect a woman they love. I realize my fears are probably more imaginary than real, but it's a place I'm in. This job can really screw you up sometimes."

"What a waste of a perfectly good appendage." Kate said with a smirk as she rolled on top of him, pressing her body firmly against his. "Well," she said in a deeper than normal voice, "Turnabout is fair play, let's see if you can make me blush."

"You're on," Brad said biting her nipple playfully.

The second round was as satisfying as the first, in different ways. When Brad asked, Kate confirmed it was blush-worthy and described a few things she hoped he'd do again.

"I just realized I forgot to eat," Brad said, "I've burned a lot of calories and need to refuel."

They moved to the bathroom for a quick shower and some foreplay they could tuck away in the backs of their minds until the next time.

In the kitchen, Kate warmed Brad's soup and crab cakes as he leaned against the counter sipping a glass of milk and watching Kate move around the kitchen in her robe and slippers.

"That robe is just the right length to drive me crazy," Brad observed, "Every time you bend over I almost get to see something, but not quite. I may shorten it an inch while you're sleeping." He came up behind her and took her in his arms while Kate stirred the soup on the stovetop.

"You sir, are becoming a dirty old man," Kate mused.

"If you have to grow old, there is no better way to do it."

Kate responded with a smile and a sarcastic "Ha, ha."

Brad ate quickly and silently, while looking up to smile at Kate as he chewed. When he finished, they decided there was no reason for Brad to sleep on the sofa sleeper.

CHAPTER 13

"**G**ood morning," Kate said to Robert as she and Brad came downstairs.

"Good morning," he said looking at the two of them with a crooked smile and a spoonful of oatmeal halfway to his mouth, "Joe has gone up to check on Delgado and take him some breakfast."

"Oh good," Kate said as she opened the refrigerator to get out the orange juice.

"I'm making breakfast," Brad whispered in her ear, "it's the least I can do for your kindness in bed this morning." He covertly patted her bottom.

Brad and Kate were sitting at the table eating a man-made breakfast of scrambled eggs, toast, bacon, and hash browns while Robert was watching a home improvement show on television. Joe came downstairs carrying Delgado's coffee mug from the previous night. As he walked past the table he made a point to sniff the mug and raise his eyebrows at Kate. "Looks like all discipline is breaking down around here," he said with a wink and a smile.

Kate pretended to ignore him. "How's Delgado?" Brad asked.

"He's not any better. I've suggested he stay in bed and have taken him some books that interest him. He says he slept pretty well though and that the tea helped him a lot," Joe looked at Kate as he said it.

"Good," Kate said, "Tell him I'll make him another cup tonight. In the meantime, there's some cough and cold medicine in the cabinet in the upstairs bathroom."

"I've already dosed him," Joe replied. They could hear Delgado coughing upstairs. "For whatever it's worth."

It was a Saturday and since Kate chose not to work on Saturday mornings, she suggested that her healthy housemates douse themselves in bug spray and join her in the raspberry patch. They spent several hours in the warm, early morning sun filling ice cream pails with ripe berries while magpies dive-bombed them in hopes of securing the fruit for themselves. "Those magpies are as annoying as mosquitoes, but not as easily discouraged. I'm starting to understand Alfred Hitchcock's motivation." Brad remarked after one grazed the top of his head and squawked loudly. "We'll leave you some, I promise," he yelled at the sky, but they remained undeterred.

They picked five heaping pails of berries and brought them into the kitchen. Kate got out a colander and started rinsing the berries while Brad and Robert went down to the basement to bring up the canning supplies Kate had ordered including jars, lids, and sugar. Joe got out a couple of baking pans and started spreading washed berries across them in a single layer. Once filled the pans would be placed into the freezer. When the berries were frozen, they would be transferred to a freezer bag. By freezing them individually on the baking pans first, they didn't stick together in the bag when they were put in the freezer for long-term storage.

By the time the men returned with all the canning supplies, Kate had a pan of boiling water rolling away on the stove. Using a pair of tongs, she carefully added the jars and lids to the boiling water to sterilize them. She repeated this process until they were all sterilized and lined up on the counter.

Meanwhile, Joe had started to whisk together and boil equal parts of raspberries and sugar. When the mixture reached the proper consistency, Kate put a canning funnel into the first jar and Joe slowly poured the sugar/berry mixture in leaving about a quarter of an inch at the top of the jar. They repeated the process until the mixture was gone. Joe rinsed the pan and started the next batch while Kate secured the lids on the jars. She then placed them on a rack in a large water-filled stockpot and slowly brought the water to a boil. The jars were allowed to boil for 10 minutes and were then removed and placed on top of a bath towel on the counter to cool. The process took most of the day, but they'd have finished jam in time for their morning toast.

That evening, Robert came downstairs with Delgado's empty food tray. "He said he would like some tea. I offered to bring him some, but he insisted that Kate make it. He said her tea is better."

"I'm sure it is," Joe said slyly, not looking up from the book he was reading.

Kate ignored Joe and took another hot toddy to Delgado, who looked terrible.

The next morning they awoke to a cold, damp cabin. The weather was changing. While it was only mid-August, in Alaska that meant fall weather was in the air. The sky was filled with dark, dense clouds and there was a steady rain hammering the metal roof. They received a message that tomorrow's supply run would be delayed at least two days due to weather. "I guess it's time to start a fire in the woodstove and warm this place up," Kate said, "Who would like to haul the first load of wood?" They had positioned about a cord of wood in the basement for easy access, but it would still need to be brought upstairs. Robert volunteered and started the fire.

"I'll get some coffee going," Brad said, rubbing his hands together.

"I'll check on Delgado to see if he needs another blanket," Joe offered.

"Who wants toast with raspberry jam?" Kate asked. All present answered in the affirmative. She made fried eggs and toast for everyone. The raspberry jam still tasted like yesterday's warm sunshine.

Delgado felt well enough to make his way downstairs after breakfast and sit in a recliner, clothed in a nightshirt and stocking cap and wrapped in a blanket. He commented that being closer to the stove might be beneficial to his condition. He reminded Kate of a character in a Victorian era novel both in his speech and mannerisms. She wondered if he put a cloth under his jaw and tied it on the top of his head when he had a toothache or regularly discussed his constitution over breakfast. Or perhaps he just reminded her of a portly Ebenezer Scrooge, 'hard and sharp as flint' as Dickens described him.

It rained for three long days during which time the group—with the exception of Delgado who preferred to brood and mutter to himself in the chair—decided to load a Russian language-learning program they found on the bookshelf into the computer. Between board games, chess, cribbage, dominos, and every imaginable card game, they learned some basic Russian and laughed at how bad at it they all seemed to be. By the second day if one more person had pointed at her and said, "You are a woman" in Russian, Kate feared she might snap their finger off.

By day three, Kate had had enough of the cabin and donned her rain gear and headed out to the garden to harvest vegetables. With a late supply plane and a garden full of fresh vegetables, there was no reason to start pulling out the canned carrots and corn; there would be plenty of that in the winter. She harvested salad greens, beans, broccoli, zucchini, and yellow squash. Joe asked her to bring in a couple of heads of cabbage because he wanted to experiment with making sauerkraut, so she cut off two generous heads. Since the weather had been cooling off, Kate had permanently moved the tomato plants into the cabin. They had started to ripen and they had an overabundance. She was going to make a large batch of spaghetti sauce that could be divided and frozen for the winter.

As Kate was getting ready to leave the garden, she smelled a strong musky odor that was a cross between a skunk and a wet dog. Then she heard it, a grunt followed by a loud nasal blow and the clacking together of teeth as the grizzly stepped out from the tall grass and alders, swinging its head back and forth, nose twitching. It lifted its nose, sniffed the air and again blew hard out its nose and clacked its teeth. The bear ambled toward the garden attracted by the smell of the wet, ripened vegetables. There was nowhere for Kate to go. The grizzly was close and approaching on the gate side of the garden. Kate latched the gate and backed into the far corner of the garden. She was a cornered animal and ready to kill.

The weight of the snub-nosed Ruger on her hip provided some comfort and she slowly withdrew it from the leather holster. The bear would have to be very close before the .357 would be effective. If it noticed her, it would charge headfirst and Kate would have to wait until the last possible moment to discharge the weapon to ensure it penetrated the bear's skull. She would have to stop it in one shot, there would be no time for another.

The grizzly stood on its hind legs and swept its head back and forth with its nose in the air breathing deeply. On his hind legs he stood about seven feet tall and while he was able to smell Kate's presence, he didn't seem to know where she was. Fortunately, the vegetables seemed to be his priority. Kate didn't make a sound. Yelling at the bear was not likely to scare it away, but would draw its attention toward Kate who, by her presence in the garden, was threatening his or her lunch. It reached out and pawed at the fence and made several short, loud growls before standing on its hind legs and pushing against a fence post. The force moved through the entire fence structure like a wave. Kate drew in her breath and exhaled slowly, she felt calm and in control of herself. *If you control your breathing, you control your body,* she told herself, *You can do this, you've practiced this scenario in your head many times. Just execute the plan.*

The post was holding and the bear fell back down on all fours. He sniffed, moved closer to the gate, and once again got on his hind legs, but this time started pushing on the fence wire. It wouldn't hold long. Kate was calculating the amount of time it would take for the bear to breach the wire when she heard a cabin window slide up quickly and Robert's voice yell, "Hey bear!" The bear dropped down to the ground, turned toward the cabin and emitted a series of grunts. He bared his teeth, put its ears back, and made a short bluff charge toward the cabin. Joe had joined at another window and was banging a wooden spoon against a pot while Robert continued yelling. The bear seemed to be backing slowly away from the garden when the door to the arctic entry opened about two inches and the barrel of the soaker water gun appeared. Brad fired and hit the bear in the face with the stream of water. The bear growled and shook its head vigorously to discharge the water. As it did, Brad hit it twice more in the ear and the neck. The bear ran toward the safety of the brush and kept going.

Kate was frozen in place, gun still at the ready. Now that the threat had passed she allowed the panic to slowly seep in, she started shaking. "Are you okay?" Brad yelled from the door. Kate nodded weakly; she was still unable to move. Brad crept slowly in her direction and spoke as if he was trying to diffuse an armed hostage situation, "It's okay. It's over. How about you lower your weapon. I'm coming toward you." Kate shook herself out of her daze, holstered her weapon and stood. She realized she had stopped shaking and the tension in her body was dissipating. Brad quickened his pace toward her. When he reached her, he hugged her tightly. "You handled that so well. How are you feeling?"

"I'm remarkably well," Kate said, "I had a moment of panic when it was over, but I recovered quite quickly. Help me bring in these vegetables, will you?"

"Of course."

"By the way, that was a much better use for that water gun than the first time you used it."

Brad chortled.

The following morning found relief from the rain and bright rays of sunshine cleared the view of Denali, though the cool temperatures persisted. The loud honking of a migrating flock of sandhill cranes brought the cabin dwellers outside with their morning coffee to watch them pass by. The supply plane would be in around 5:00 and Brad asked to be dropped off at his truck after lunch for the more than 3-hour drive back to the military base before heading back to DC. Kate suggested they take their lunch in the foothills of the Alaska Range so they could pick some blueberries. "You just want to get me alone for a while," Brad quipped.

"Who could blame a girl," Kate replied. While they didn't know it at the time, lunch in the foothills would become their ritual every time Brad had to leave the cabin. They left early so they could pick blueberries before lunch. With their buckets full, Kate spread out a tarp to protect their blanket from the wet ground. Brad sat down and grabbed Kate's arm and pulled her on top of him. "Picking berries doesn't work up much of an appetite, but I know an activity that does," he moaned as he kissed her firmly and squeezed the inside of her right thigh. Kate did not protest and they made love in the clean, cool air as a ray of sunshine peeked out from behind the mountain. They didn't bother to dress before they ate their lunch; they just wrapped the blanket around themselves.

After dropping the berries at the cabin, Brad joined Kate on her ATV and she drove him to his truck. He kissed her and with little fanfare and a wave, drove away. Kate sighed and mounted the ATV with a sense of loss.

At 5:00, Kate and Joe made their way to the supply plane. Much to Kate's surprise, Brad was on the flight. "I got back to base before the plane left and thought I would surprise you." He hugged her.

"Consider me surprised!" Kate said.

"I brought something for everyone," he said enthusiastically as he handed Kate a bundle wrapped in white butcher paper. "It's four pounds of king crab legs. I thought everyone could use a treat, plus I'm hoping Delgado is allergic to shellfish."

"How can anyone be so mean and so thoughtful all at the same time? Whatever possessed you?"

"I know fresh crab is one of your favorite things about living in Alaska and since you're stuck out here, I thought it would be a nice treat. Uncle Sam will spring for surround sound, but for some reason not crab. Enjoy." Brad kissed her and hopped back up in the co-pilot's seat.

As Kate cooked the crab for everyone in the cabin that night, her sense of loss was replaced by contentment.

Chapter 14

The next morning Kate sequestered herself in the communication room as usual to work on her research project. She hadn't done any work during Brad's visit and the break was refreshing and she returned to work with renewed enthusiasm. She opened the spreadsheets and looked at the work she had done, checked her formulas and correlations, and continued her online research to look for variables she had missed. After two hours, she was feeling frustrated again.

The stool Kate sat on to do her work was stuck at a height that didn't allow her feet to touch the floor. It had been difficult to adjust the first time and since no one else used it Kate had forgotten to lubricate it as she planned. When Brad used the communication room he must have raised the stool and now it appeared frozen at that setting. She tried again to adjust it, but the lever was ineffective in lowering the height. Perhaps she and Joe could take it apart later and try to fix it. A spider ran across the floor and Kate instinctively stomped on it and shuddered. She was not a fan of arachnids in any of their forms.

Feeling like she was four years old again, Kate sat on the stool and swung her legs as she stared at the computer screen not knowing what to do next. She was kicking something rhythmically with her right foot. *Thump, thump, thump.* Eventually she looked down to see what she was abusing. It was the metal box containing Max's things. Kate slid off the stool and onto the floor. She pulled the box toward her and out from under the desk. Sitting back on her heels, she looked at the box and ran her hand over the top. *Yes,* she thought, *I think I might be strong enough to open it now.*

Slowly, Kate pulled the chain that held the key out from under her shirt and over her head, never taking her eyes off the box. She held the key as she tried to convince herself to put it in the lock. *What's in there? Will I be able to handle it?* she wondered. "I should have asked Brad about the contents," she said aloud to the room and whatever insects might be listening. Impulsively, Kate suddenly thrust the key into the lock, turned it, and threw open the lid. "There, you survived that," Kate mumbled to herself. She was doing better than the spider so far.

The box was only half full and the first thing she saw was an official-looking file folder with an FBI seal and case number. She set it on the floor and opened it. On the top of the file was a sheet of photo paper that contained four of what must have been the crime scene photos taken by the authorities in Singapore. She closed her eyes and gasped as she slammed the file folder closed. "Oh shit, oh shit, oh shit," Kate said aloud as she tried to normalize her breathing. "Okay, get ahold of yourself. You've seen them, you can look at them again." Her heart was beating so hard she could feel her blood pulsing throughout her entire body. Kate slowly opened the folder and looked more closely at the photos. She knew they were pictures of Max, but it was somewhat difficult for her to tell. The body was bloated, his face was abnormally red, and the one eye she could see clearly appeared to be badly swollen. Max's head was positioned at an awkward angle that implied his neck had probably been broken. The navy blue pants and denim shirt he wore were not his, as far as Kate knew, and they appeared to be wet. His feet were bare. His right shirtsleeve was torn and although it was badly distorted due to the bloating, Kate could see the wing of an eagle tattoo Max had gotten in Guam when he was in the Marines.

Kate went to take a deep breath and realized her right hand was clamped over her mouth. She put her hand down to her side and wiggled her fingers to try to release the stony sensation that had set into them. She turned the photo sheet over and looked at the next item in the file.

There were about ten pages of interviews with people who had seen Max the day before he disappeared and there didn't appear to be any helpful comments in them. Next were photos of Max's hotel room that showed no sign of struggle or distress. Max's personal effects had been given to Kate after his death, but she looked closely at the photos to see if there was anything in the room that hadn't been given to her. Nothing stood out. The final group of papers contained the official report by the Singapore police. They listed the cause of death as "Accidental Drowning" and that there were "no signs of foul play". Kate wasn't a medical doctor, but even she could tell by the photos that the likelihood of his death having been caused by drowning was pretty slim. It seemed odd to her that there was no autopsy report in the file, even though it was referenced in the official police report.

Kate set the file aside and looked into the box. The only other thing in the box was a stack of 12 by 8 ½ inch continuous form computer paper with holes on the sides used to slip over the pins in the printer to feed it through. She reached in and pulled out the stack. The stack was actually four separate documents. The first three appeared to be schematics, each about twenty pages long, mapping some type of process, workflow, or system. The fourth was about 3 inches thick and looked to Kate to be a printout of a complicated computer program of some type. She started to read it, but quickly became lost in the branching.

With the program printout in hand, Kate left the communication room, locked the door, and walked to her bedroom. She set the printout on the desk, opened the right hand drawer, and moved things around until she found some dry erase markers. She drew a small rectangle on the whiteboard and wrote "Enter" inside it. She added two lines to indicate the branches the program took. Above the first she wrote "If Stock" and wrote "If Currency" over the second. To the end of each of the two branch lines she added another two branches where she placed rectangles that said "Exchange" and "Dark Pool". Kate spent the rest of the next couple of hours slowly working on mapping the computer program, but it soon became obvious it was too large and complex to fit on the whiteboard. She brought in her laptop and transferred her work onto it. She wiped off the whiteboard and locked both the papers and her laptop back in the communications room.

Chapter 15

Summer had quickly turned to fall at the cabin and Kate had finished harvesting the last of the carrots and potatoes a month earlier. Fortunately for everyone Delgado's stay had been short as the powers that be decided the remote location was not a good fit for him. By the time he left most in the cabin didn't care if he was turned over to the enemy, as long as he was gone. Brad was making it to the cabin once a month or so and was two days into his October visit. Halloween was in four days, Robert had left a week ago and a man named Everett had joined them. Kate continued her work, but had given up looking for correlations, and spent her time trying to decode the large document she found in Max's box. An intricate stock and currency-trading algorithm of some sort was beginning to emerge from the computer code.

They had been receiving intermittent light snow over the past two weeks and Kate decided it was time to move her truck to the Amber Creek parking lot for the winter. Kate had used the satellite phone to call the State Troopers to report the make, model, and license plate number of the truck so they knew it belonged to a year-round resident and where her cabin was in case they needed to contact her. Doing so would ensure they didn't launch a search and rescue mission for the missing owner or tow it. She also posted a notice on the inside of the windshield—whatever good it would do once the snow covered it.

Since Everett had come in on the plane and had never been to the parking lot, he volunteered to follow Kate's truck on the ATV. He had not brought a warm hat with him to the cabin, but had managed to find a Yankees stocking cap that Robert had left behind in his locker in the entryway. While Robert was probably unhappy to find it missing, Everett was grateful to have it on his head while riding down the trail at thirty miles per hour in the cold fall air. Everett had said, based on what he knew about recent deployments, Robert wouldn't need it where he was anyway.

After dropping off the truck, Kate and Everett directed the ATV toward the airstrip to pick up the riding lawnmower. It would have to be brought back to the shed to be winterized and stored until spring. The ground was already frozen and it was a good time to drive the riding mower across the trail before it was covered in snow. Once they deposited the lawnmower into the shed, they attached the snowplow to the front of one of the ATVs. The goal was to keep the grass strip plowed as long as they could so supply planes could continue to land. Once the snow started falling heavily, they would no longer be able to keep up with the plowing and supplies would start being dropped in by helicopter.

Kate and Everett arrived back at the cabin to find Joe in a recliner reading *The Complete Sherlock Holmes*. He looked up and greeted them when they arrived. Kate sat on the sofa and asked Joe how he was enjoying the book. She had recommended it to him.

"I'm enjoying it very much," he said, " While I've seen the modern adaptations of the stories, it's always good to return to the original literature. On a philosophical note, do you think we all have a Moriarty in our lives? What I mean is, a person who respects you and your intellect, but feels they must destroy you in some way to retain their life's purpose, yet they end up destroying themselves, either in whole or part, at the same time?"

"That's a deep question, but I suspect it is possible that at some level a Moriarty exists for all of us."

"I feel like there was a professor on my dissertation committee who may have been my Moriarty," Joe reflected. "My research came to different conclusions than his, and while he always seemed to have respect for my academic credibility, he tried to prevent me from publishing my findings and ended up destroying his reputation at the same time."

"I didn't know you had a doctorate," Kate said "Do you care to tell me what field it is in?"

"I will have to decline," Joe said smiling and shaking his head, "I have probably already shared too much as it is."

"I understand," Kate said returning his smile, "That is an interesting example, but I'm not sure a Moriarty has arisen in my life yet."

"I fear your Moriarty will emerge, as I think it does for all of us at some point." Joe looked deeply thoughtful, "Just remember, when he does show up in your life, whatever your Moriarty does to you, he or she will be harming themselves perhaps more than they are harming you." Joe frowned and sighed, "I wish it was not one of life's rites of passage, but it is unfortunately necessary to our formation as a person."

"What did you take away from your Moriarty experience?" Kate asked.

"Nothing positive from an ideal life perspective I suppose. I learned to trust other people less, become more careful about forming alliances, and I've retreated into myself a little more and share less about my work and myself. I became less of an idealist and more of a realist. I think the shift to realism was the rite of passage it primarily represented for me. So, enjoy your idealism while you can, I often miss it." Joe frowned and went back to reading his book. Kate felt a pang of pity for him and her future self as well.

Kate crept upstairs to find Brad napping on her bed, snoring lightly, eyes twitching under his eyelids. She didn't wish to disturb him, so she quietly opened the communications room door and went in. While she had been working to understand what the large computer program in Max's box, Kate hadn't paid much attention to the smaller documents that contained the schematics. She sat down on the floor and pulled them out of the box. This time she noticed the first one had "Silverberg" handwritten sideways across the top right corner. She looked at the others and found they were labeled "P.D. Welch" and "LiquiFlow". Silverberg and P.D. Welch were large global investment banks, while LiquiFlow was a leading operator of securities markets owning three major electronic stock exchanges. All three companies were major players in the financial industry, each transacting millions of trades each day.

Kate studied the Silverberg schematic first. While it had made no sense to her the first time she saw it, her work on the computer code in the large document helped her make sense of what she was looking at. It appeared to be a schematic of Silverberg's stock order flow process including everything from how and where they entered orders to how they were routed to exchanges. It even included the details of three of the trading algorithms they use to trade large orders of stock.

"Wait a minute," Kate said aloud standing up to grab her laptop off the desk. She sat back down on the floor and opened the schematic of the large computer program she was working on. While the program had a significant number of branches, one of the branches she had worked part of the way through looked similar to the Silverberg schematic. It took her a while to find what she was looking for, but when she did, she held the Silverberg schematic next to her computer. The large program had a branch that looked like it entered into a program identical to the Silverberg order flow system, at least as far as she had mapped it. The point were it looked like the Silverberg system may have been accessed was simply labeled "Enter 105059" in the notes on the code. Could it be the Silverberg system? "Son of a bitch!" Kate exclaimed louder than she should have.

There was a gentle knock on the door and Brad said, "Kate, is everything okay?" Kate got up and opened the door to let Brad in.

"You need to see this," she said with urgency. Brad sat down beside her and Kate explained what she had found.

"So do you think the sizeable program you're decoding is a larger part of Silverberg's trading system?" Brad asked.

"I don't know yet, I still have a lot to decode. The program is very complex." Kate picked up the other two schematics and paged through them, "These don't look familiar to me, so maybe the large program is something designed for Silverberg. But why would it be part of Max's investigation? I don't think MAK Software ever did any business with Silverberg, but I'll ask on the next conference call. The other thing I'm going to need to do is work through the math in these trading algorithms to figure out what they do. It will take me a while."

"Good thing you have a long winter ahead of you," Brad pecked her on the cheek. "Why don't you pack this stuff up, Joe has made pulled pork sandwiches, homemade coleslaw, and beans for dinner."

"That sounds like a great incentive to quit working! I'll be right down."

Joe's pulled pork sandwiches were incredible. Kate had no idea how he pulled off smoky and sweet pork in a slow cooker. She would forever be ashamed to serve hers, which was bland by comparison.

Everett smoked a pipe, so even though the temperature had gotten quite cold, the group had started retiring to the screened porch after dinner so Everett could smoke. To keep them warm, Joe had fashioned a fire pit for the deck using the bottom third of a metal barrel he had found on the property and legs he had fabricated out of aluminum in the shop. It wasn't pretty, but it was functional. To increase their warmth, the quartet sipped warm brandy that Brad had smuggled to the cabin. Though alcohol other than beer and wine was not formally allowed at the cabin, they had found brandy snifters on the top shelf of a cabinet in the kitchen. Kate suspected Brad had something to do with that too.

Everett smoked a Meerschaum pipe, intricately carved into an eagle's head. After Joe got the fire going and sat back in his chair rubbing his hands together near the flames he asked, "You don't see many pipe smokers anymore, what brought you to it?"

"My mother worked for the State Department and when I was 16, we moved to a station in Germany. I used to go into the smoke shops with friends to enjoy the aroma of the cigars and pipe tobaccos in the walk-in humidors. Occasionally I'd buy a cigar, but while the scent of tobacco appealed to me, I always felt loutish with a cigar in my mouth. A pipe seemed more respectable so eventually I bought myself a basic pipe and started experimenting with different tobaccos. A German friend's parents bought me a Meerschaum pipe for my high school graduation and I was amazed at how the flavor of the tobacco was enhanced by the pipe. I have been hooked ever since, so to speak." Everett took four short puffs on the pipe as he lit the tobacco with a stick he had set alight from the fire pit.

Kate huddled near the fire and stared into the flames with a distant look, still thinking about what she had discovered today. Aware of her state, Brad poked her playfully in the side. "I'm going to keep poking you until you relax," he said. Kate became conscious of what she was doing and shook off her trance.

"Look at that sunset," Joe said jerking his chin toward the sky. The sun had dipped just below the horizon and a pink and orange alpenglow illuminated the mountains and charged red the patches of thin, wispy cirrus clouds. Fall was Kate's favorite time of year in Alaska. Summer's continuous sun robbed them of sunsets and fall meant an end to the relentless attacks of bugs. Delgado had no idea what he was missing.

Chapter 16

By Thanksgiving, winter was in full force. They had managed to keep the airstrip plowed, but it was becoming increasingly difficult as winter winds were causing blowing and drifting snow. Keeping warm became their number one priority and they took shifts stoking the wood stove. Temperatures had been in the low 20s during the day and were dropping into the teens at night. The Toyo heater did help keep the cabin warm at night, but not warm enough to be comfortable in the morning. Kate had also added a pot of water to the top of the stove, which put moisture into the air to counteract the drying effects of the wood stove that was causing the cabin's inhabitants to fight nosebleeds.

Kate had ordered all the fixings for a traditional Thanksgiving dinner and the turkey was slowing roasting in the oven, filling the cabin with smells that reminded everyone of home. Brad had arrived yesterday to spend a four-day weekend with the group and Everett would be leaving with Brad on Monday. Kate and Joe would be alone in the cabin for a while, since no other guests where scheduled to come in.

They were only getting about 5 hours of daylight each day, so the supply flights had started coming in at noon when the light was best. The cabin was receiving no direct sunlight anymore as the sun never rose high enough to clear the mountains that surrounded them in the valley. The days were grey and gloomy and the nights were long.

To overcome the weather, Kate threw herself into her work. Joe and Everett seemed to have a more difficult time managing their cabin fever. Joe tried to get outside during the brightest part of the day and chop wood and Everett joined him in the daily snow removal necessitated by the blowing and drifting snow even on days when no fresh snow fell. Kate noticed that Joe spent more time running on the treadmill than he had in the past to ward off the stress that being cooped up was causing.

Kate had told the men about the Alaskan tradition of learning something new each winter and suggested they each learn a new skill. Joe had taken up pastry making and was spending some of his time creating elaborate and complicated desserts. This led to Kate spending more time on the treadmill as well. Everett had decided he wanted to learn to knit, but didn't want the others in the cabin to tell anyone. Once he learned, he knitted scarves for Brad, Kate, and Joe and spent the rest of his time working on a wool afghan to take home with him. Only he would know the whole story behind it and, for better or worse, it would remind him of his time at the cabin.

Perhaps it was the short days or cabin fever, but the conversations on the radio had migrated from issues like recycling and whether the town should install streetlights to more bizarre and unusual topics. Tonight's show was no exception. Many of the regular radio hosts appeared to be gone this week and a man named Gene, whom most of the callers seemed to know, was hosting tonight's community comment program.

"Yeah Gene, it's Frank, it was good to see you at the potluck last week. Tell Betty we enjoyed the chicken casserole. The reason for my call is that last night about one o'clock in the morning I saw some strange lights in the sky out toward the north part of town. There were about ten lights in a v-shape, and it looked like something very large was flying over because behind the lights it was black and you couldn't see the stars. There must have been a large solid object there to smudge out the stars like that. The vehicle looked to be rectangular in shape and then pointed at the front where the lights were. I'm just wondering if anyone else saw it."

"Hi Gene, it's Urbie, I agree with the last caller, Betty's casserole was great and my wife wants the recipe if she's willing to give it up. You know, I didn't see what your last caller saw last night, but I'm also concerned about what's going on in the Alaskan skies at night. When it's dark like this, it makes it easier for the government to fly over and drop chemicals on us. They've been using these chemical trails to distribute all sorts of stuff to people. I don't know if they are trying to sterilize us, or poison us, or if they're running some kind of physical or mind experiments. I don't know why there aren't more investigations into these things. I've talked to our U.S. representatives, but I think they are complicit in the whole thing because they refuse to launch an investigation.

"Happy Thanksgiving Gene. I agree, Betty's casserole was great, but did you try that broccoli salad? It was incredible. If anyone knows who made it, let me know so I can get the recipe. I did see what your first caller saw last night, but your second caller got me thinking. What if the lights your first caller saw were just the lights from a regular commercial airplane, but he couldn't see the stars behind it because the government was spreading chemicals from it, which obliterated the view of the stars?"

Kate looked at Brad, "Were you spreading chemicals on us last night?"

With a false sincerity that emitted sarcasm, Brad raised his fork in the air and declared, "I can neither confirm nor deny that anyone within the government was spreading chemicals on persons known or unknown last night. But if they were, I would have suggested that they start at the homes of the first two callers."

Everyone chuckled before Brad continued, "So gentleman, let's use a little tradecraft and analyze the last caller, what did you hear?"

"He's a much smarter man than the others which makes him feel superior. I think he was demonstrating his superiority, by evoking seriousness in his call, when he was really just making fun of the first two callers," Joe said, never missing a bite of his mashed potatoes.

"I agree with Joe's analysis, but would add that he was also making fun of the host. I'm willing to bet there was no broccoli salad at the potluck," Everett added.

"Very good," Brad said, "but I'm also willing to bet that he did see the same 'UFO' the first caller saw and was originally calling in to explain what it was. However, after hearing the second caller he made up his mind that these people are just too naive to accept the realities of what it was and decided to make fun of them instead." All three men nodded in agreement.

Kate decided the only thing that separated the three men at her table from the last caller was that they decided to show their intellectual superiority over the most intelligent caller, rather than the most vulnerable. She excused it as boredom and a need for mental stimulation.

As someone who had started to feel like the odd person out in her academic field, Kate strangely appreciated living near people who weren't afraid to speak their minds, no matter how crazy they may seem to others. Kate was aware that many academics thought there was something wrong with her free-market, minimal regulation thinking, so who was she to judge. She feared she might be developing empathy.

That night Kate was grateful not only for the sex that Brad provided, but also his body heat under the covers. "You're so warm," she said getting as close to him as possible.

"Good heart," Brad said, "pumps a lot of blood. We probably need to send out some heated blankets or something though." They lay silently together each deep in their own thoughts as Kate stroked Brad's chest hair and a nearby owl persistently asked, *"Who, who?".*

On Sunday the wind was gusting to about twenty miles per hour and there was light snow. They got word in the morning that the supply plane was still going to attempt to come in. Everett, who was anxious to get home, spent most of the morning riding a snowmachine back and forth from the cabin to the airstrip to run the plow over the landing strip and keep it free of as much snow as possible. Brad and Kate decided to skip their traditional pre-departure lunch in the foothills.

Watching the plane land was gut wrenching. As it approached, the plane appeared to be straight and level, but wobbling just a bit as the pilot struggled against the significant crosswinds. As it got ready to land, a windshear caused the right wing of the plane to pitch upward and the plane to turn about twenty degrees to the runway. The pilot kept the plane in the air as long as he could and managed to straighten it out, but had to land farther down the short airstrip than usual. He skidded down the snowy strip and succeeded in stopping the plane just before he hit the fence at the end. The pilot hopped out and ran around to look at the front of the plane. With his hands on his hips he said, "That was close. Well kids, I think we're done coming in here by plane until spring. Time to let the chopper do some work."

The group got to work unloading the plane and once it was empty, they helped push the plane backwards and turn it around. Before he boarded, Brad turned to Kate and kissed her warmly, his face softening and his eyes drooping, "I really think I have to tell you…I think…I…I…" he paused, took a deep breath and swallowed hard to regain control of himself, "I'm going to miss you at the very least," he said. Kate wondered what he really wanted to say.

Chapter 17

Kate and Joe were still the only residents of the cabin by mid-December. The weather had turned bitterly cold with temperatures reaching twenty below zero at night and the high never made it above zero during the day. Inside the cabin, the windows and door handles were covered in ice every morning when they got up. By mid-morning, with a hot enough fire in the stove, they could usually get the interior ice to melt.

With little to do, Kate would wrap up in her goose down comforter and sit on the floor of the communications room most of the day mapping the computer program. It had become an obsession fueled by cabin fever. She had started to print sections of the schematic she was creating and was taping them in sequence around the room. The program currently rapped around the room three times. She was making notes in red ink on the pages indicating entry and exit points into different trading systems and, as she got near the end, different exchanges. In addition to an entry into the Silverburg program, she had eventually run into links to the P.D. Welch and LiquiFlow schematics and labeled those. There were many other links that appeared to go from other trading firms to other exchanges, but she had no indication which firms they were. Today was the day Kate was determined to finish decoding.

This morning, still in her pajamas and wrapped in her comforter, Kate went downstairs early, stoked the fire, and ate some breakfast. She wrapped both hands tightly around her coffee mug and hovered over it to capture the heat from the steam on her cold nose. She feared she might never be truly warm again as she watched the ice at the inside edges of the window slowly start to thin and produce droplets of water that rolled toward the sill. At least something was thawing.

The thought of the cold transition from comforter to shower made Kate skip the shower and stay as she was. She was in the communication room working before Joe got up. Two hours later there was a light knock on the door. "Kate, are you in there?" Kate opened the door to find Joe standing there with a serious look on his face.

"I'm here," Kate said suddenly aware that her hair was probably sticking out all over as it always did before she showered.

"Oh good. I just wanted to make sure you weren't lost outside somewhere. Sorry to disturb you," Joe said as he pulled the door closed.

Kate went back to work for the rest of the day breaking twice for food and the bathroom. By one o'clock the following morning, she had reached the last page of code. As she read through it, she saw something that caused her to momentarily freeze. When she recovered, Kate stood up and started pacing small circles within the confines of the tiny room. "No, no, no," she whispered aloud, "it can't be."

Included in all sections of code in a computer program, between double backslashes, are comments that explain what the code in that section does. The purpose is to ensure that other programmers have an explanation of what the intent of the code is or to help debug code that is not working as intended. To Kate's astonishment, the last three comments on the page were:

\\February 3rd\\
\\Kate\\
\\I love you\\

It was dated nearly a month before they had found Max's body. How could that be? What was this program? Kate frantically decoded the last short page, added it to the wall, and started looking at the program from the beginning and circling around the room three times to the end over and over again. She occasionally made marks on the pages with her red pen. *Code, program, trading, stock, markets, exchanges, routing, orders....* "I don't get it!" she yelled at the wall, "What the hell were you up to Max? Damn you!"

At six in the morning it clicked. *Holy shit, this is bad. Max, how could you do this?* Kate sat on the floor with tears streaming down her face from anger and exhaustion. Several minutes later, she pulled herself up onto the stool and with renewed determination lifted the laptop from the floor to the desk and started searching for information on several stocks. When she was done, she opened her email and sent a secure message to Brad, requesting very specific U.S. market information on fifteen particular stocks and asked him to randomly select an additional fifteen.

As she came out of the communication room, Joe was coming out of his bedroom. "Have you been to bed?" he asked.

"No, I'm going there now" Kate said mechanically, walking past Joe without looking at him. She collapsed onto her bed and slept for twelve hours.

That evening, Kate stumbled downstairs feeling like she had a hangover. Joe was sitting at the dining table reading a book, surrounded by evidence of a dinner of leftover chicken and dumplings. "If you'll forgive me, you look terrible," Joe observed. "Your lips are all dry and shriveled, when was the last time you had anything to drink?"

"I don't know," Kate croaked hoarsely.

"Sit down, let me get you some water." Kate drank it eagerly, distinctly aware of her thirst once the first drop touched her throat. She could already feel the headache diminishing.

"What's wrong?" Joe asked with his eyebrows pressed low and together in a gesture of genuine concern.

"I can't talk about it," Kate's voice lacked inflection.

"Okay, most of us here can't talk about our work, I get it, but we can at least talk about how we're feeling. So, what's going on with you emotionally?" Joe asked with sensitivity.

"I feel stunned, betrayed, angry, sad, and I'm reevaluating whether my life is and has been what I've always thought it was. The irony is, at the same time I'm having a difficult time caring about much of anything, including whether it's even worth the emotions I'm pouring into it."

Joe watched Kate closely, "Okay. Good. Let's talk about that a bit. First, if you're feeling betrayed I imagine it is because the actions of someone close to you have put you in this state...which I suspect might be Brad...or Max." Kate felt her right eyebrow involuntarily twitch at the mention of Max's name.

Joe chose his words carefully, "If the person who, shall we say, committed this crime against your emotional state is Max, it would be quite natural to feel stunned since he was such a big part of your life, someone you knew so well for so long...and...and now you feel like he's done something outside his character perhaps?" He waited. Kate sighed heavily. "I would just remind you, that sometimes things are not what they seem at first glance so don't let your emotions blind you. Second, you would also be angry, but...perhaps at yourself for not seeing the 'crime' or knowing it was coming. And finally, your propensity toward not caring might indicate your realization that, again assuming Max is the culprit, you can't confront him about it."

Kate shrugged. She had said all she was capable of saying at the moment.

Joe asked, "Since you can't confront Max, you need to ask yourself if there are any actions you can take that will make things better for you, and if not, you may need to just let it go. I would also suggest that if this issue is related to your work, you should probably step away from it for a while for perspective. In the meantime, I need to get you something to eat." He got up and headed toward the kitchen.

Kate ate without tasting and could feel a wave of weariness washing over her again. She forced herself to stay up and watch television until ten o'clock and then told Joe she was going to turn in.

About an hour later, Joe quietly opened the door to Kate's room and stuck his head in. She was asleep on her back and breathing heavily. He walked silently to the communications room, inserted a key into the lock, and let himself in. Joe turned on the light and glanced briefly around the room at what Kate had done. He picked up the secure satellite phone and dialed a number.

"Carlo's Pizza, will this be for pickup or delivery?" the person answering the call asked.

Joe said two words, "She's hot," and pressed the phone's off button.

CHAPTER 18

It took Kate about three days to start coming out of her malaise. She had started to realize that until Brad arrived with the information she requested, there was little she could do to prove or disprove her theory and dwelling on it wouldn't help. Joe also helped distract her by trying to give her other, more positive things to think about. Around mid-afternoon, Joe went outside to chop some wood. Shortly thereafter, Kate heard someone kicking the door to the arctic entryway. When she looked out, she saw Joe holding up a small pine tree with both hands, a wide smile stretching across his face. Kate opened the door and the scent of pine filled the room as Joe dragged the tree in. "Merry Christmas," he said, "I thought we should have a tree for the holidays. I hoped it might help improve your mood. Just because one chapter of your life has closed, it doesn't mean a new on can't open."

"What a great idea," Kate said, smiling pleasantly, "Thank you."

Kate was reminded again that Joe was a good man and she hadn't quite figured out how to return his kindnesses. Joe was one of those people who always seemed to know exactly what to do and say in every situation. Few people did. As Kate considered herself hopelessly socially awkward, she always admired that characteristic in him. They had been living together for almost seven months now, but other than what he ate for breakfast and what he liked to read, she still knew very little about him. He struck Kate as a man of strong character, intelligence, and discipline. He was controlled and deliberate in everything he did and said.

Even though guests were briefed that Kate wasn't a 'comfort girl', some still tried to seduce her in more traditional ways. Joe, on the other hand, had never even looked at Kate in an inappropriate manner. Kate imagined him to be married with three kids. The kind of guy who looked at his family photo each night and kissed it before going to sleep. His wife was lucky to have him and he was probably anxious to get home, yet he showed little, if any, signs of stress or anxiety.

Joe improvised a tree stand using a bucket and some rocks and Kate guided him, with a series of "A little to the left" or "A little to the right", toward vertical alignment. Kate popped some popcorn and the two of them spent the rest of the day making popcorn garland and reminiscing about their childhood Christmases. The next day they cut cardboard into two-dimensional ornament shapes: round, teardrop, icicle, star, candy cane, and gingerbread men. They covered the cardboard with foil, poked a hole through the top of each, and used dental floss to hang them from the tree. The silver ornaments sparkled in the firelight coming from the glass front of the wood stove.

"We need something to put on top," Joe said scratching his chin and knitting his brows like he was trying to solve a complicated equation.

"Hmmm...I don't have a good idea," Kate said, "I guess we can think about it."

"I suppose we don't have to decide right now," Joe said.

That evening on the radio they listened to the local residents meander through a series of debates about the validity of recent Big Foot sightings in the woods to the east of the 'Old Grantham Place just off Fireweed Road', speculation about how 'Old Man Grantham' made his money, and whether the Grantham house was really haunted or just occupied by runaway teenagers.

Following the community speculation and rumor mill program, the announcer reported, "Don't forget, every weekend over the next few months, weather permitting, the Air National Guard will be conducting drills during daylight hours in the Trapper Creek area. So, don't be alarmed by any loud noises, vehicles, or low flying aircraft in the area."

"Oh good, it sounds like we'll be getting fresh bananas tomorrow so I think I'll eat the last one," Joe said over his shoulder as he walked toward the kitchen. "When's Brad coming?" he asked returning to the great room holding an overly ripe banana with two bites already missing.

"When he left he said he'd try to be here by the twenty-third, but he doesn't tell me if his plans change. He pretty much comes when he is able and, since we live in isolation, I welcome the surprise."

"I like Brad," Joe said, "He's a solid guy. How do you feel about him?" He raised his eyebrows up and down rapidly after he asked. Kate half expected him to break into a singsong taunt about Brad and Kate sitting in a tree K-I-S-S-I-N-G, but he refrained.

"I find him to be a solid guy as well and I'm sure Brad would concur with our assessment," Kate threw Joe a crooked smile before sticking her tongue out at him. Two could play grade school games. Before Joe could say anything else, Kate bounded up the stairs to climb into bed with Homer and his *Odyssey*, a poor substitute for Brad and his...embrace.

The following morning was cloudless and the sun rose by 10:15 and it would set by 3:30 this afternoon. In the air you could see the glint of tiny bits of fluffy snow being lifted on a light breeze. By 11:00, Kate and Joe heard the sounds of F-22 Raptors dogfighting overhead. They pulled on boots, snow pants, coats, hats, and gloves to go out and watch the airshow. The maneuvers the F-22s could do and the tight pattern within which they were able to execute the dogfight were amazing. There were a total of three fighters, two of them chasing the other. After about thirty minutes, the two chase fighters left and the remaining F-22 appeared to sit motionless in the air before speeding up, executing a J-turn and flying out of sight.

As the sound of the Raptors faded, the distant chopping patter of a helicopter could be heard and soon they could see it in the distance, a load of supplies dangling precariously from a pallet slung under its belly. Once overhead, they could hear the relentless whine of the rotors and the fluttering roar of air moving across the blades. The pilots slowly lowered the supplies toward the ground, careful not to clip any of the nearby trees as Kate signaled them to keep coming. It was nearly impossible so see the pallet once it got within twenty feet of the ground as the wind generated by the helicopter was churning up the snow, but Kate could hear a whoosh and feel a thud as it hit the snow and threw the pilot a fist signal to stop. Joe ran as quickly as he could in the knee deep, swirling snow to release the large carabiner attaching the pallet to the haul rope. Once he did, he ran back and gave the pilots a 'thumbs-up'. The co-pilot returned the signal as the helicopter added power and slowly rose while someone inside began reeling in the haul line.

Kate went to get the sled they usually towed behind the snow machine and brought it to the pallet. Since Kate was considerably shorter than Joe, the snow went nearly all the way up her legs and walking was slow and difficult. She would have to remember to use the snowshoes next time and she and Joe would need to ride the snow machines across the area to pack down the snow and make it easier to walk on. They loaded about half the supplies into the sled and climbed into the rope loop at the front and began pulling, like two underpowered mules, toward the cabin. Once they got to the base of the stairs, they unloaded the sled into the arctic entryway and went back for the rest. By the time they had moved everything inside the cabin they were exhausted and half frozen. They left the supplies on the floor and went to the fire to warm themselves.

"You have frost on your eye lashes and eyebrows," Kate said pointing at Joe's face.

"So do you!" That explained why her eyes felt sticky when she blinked. "I think there is frost in my sinuses too," Joe declared, "I need to wear a facemask next time."

"I swear," Kate said, right hand raised as if to take an oath, "I will never complain about the temperature in the cabin again."

"I guess we have to do that again next week, don't we?" Joe observed, "I'm not sure it's worth it for a Christmas ham."

"I, for one, would crawl over glass for a honey-glazed spiral cut ham and some cheesy scalloped potatoes," Kate said.

"I didn't know there would be cheesy potatoes, that changes everything," Joe said emphatically as he poked Kate in the shoulder for punctuation.

Kate and Joe had finally thawed enough that they could get their outerwear off and start putting away the supplies. "It's going to be a week before this toilet paper touches my behind," Kate said thumping it against the wall to demonstrate it's frozen state. "We could, however, pound nails with it if we had a need."

"Well here's a problem," Joe said holding up a bunch of bananas like a victorious monkey, "The bananas are frozen. They'll just be mush when they thaw."

"No worries," Kate said taking the bananas from Joe and putting them into the freezer, "when I was a kid we used to eat frozen bananas dipped in chocolate. I guess that's how we'll eat these. We're probably going to have to revise our supply list though, taking into consideration that everything will spend time hanging from a helicopter in sub-zero temperatures. We'll be eating less fresh produce and more canned and frozen."

"I suppose we'll survive," Joe said.

That evening, Kate and Joe were dipping frozen bananas in Hershey's syrup for dessert and listening to the radio announcements.

"To Yukon Jim: We're going to do a flag stop on the train and come out to your place for Christmas. We'll bring all the food and drinks so you won't have to worry about anything. We miss you and we'll see you Christmas Eve. Mom, Dad, Uncle Tony, and Aunt Midge."

"To Shoes: There are a couple of packages for you sitting at the post office with your regular mail. If you can't get in to pick it up, I'll send it with someone going your way, since that's what you've asked me to do in the past. If that's not what you want, please get in contact. From the Talkeetna Postmaster."

"To Out There Jane: There will be two of us coming out for Christmas. We'll arrive noon on the twenty-second."

"Sounds like we might be getting another guest," Kate said.

"Yes, and Brad's using it as an excuse to come a day early," Joe wiggled his eyebrows up and down again and smirked. Kate wiggled hers back at him. She was, after all, quite excited to see Brad and the data he would hopefully bring with him.

Chapter 19

On the twenty-second, Joe and Kate met Brad and a man he introduced as Shadow in the Amber Creek parking lot. They were bundled up in so many clothes, Kate could only tell that Shadow appeared to be of average height, maybe five foot ten inches with steady, brown eyes. She had not been aware of any of the other guest's eye color, but when that's the only identifying feature available to you, you notice. Kate hoped she wouldn't have to pick him out of a lineup or identify his body before she had more information.

The two of them loaded a bag each into the sled and Shadow insisted on holding a long rectangular case in his lap on the ride back to the cabin. Kate guessed Shadow was a sniper, or more specifically, an Agency assassin. He was the first person Kate deeply perceived had a reason for being at a safe house. He was no accountant; he was a highly skilled killer. While she could only see Shadow's eyes, they communicated much and Kate intuitively had a sense of him. The case, Kate speculated, contained his best rifle and it never left his side, not even in the middle of nowhere amongst friends. Sometimes that's where you were the most vulnerable. Kate suddenly felt the urge to look around and behind her as they sped off toward the cabin with Brad holding onto her from behind. Shadow had brought with him a sense of uneasiness that descended upon Kate like the inky darkness of an Alaska night.

At the cabin, Joe took Shadow upstairs to show him his room while Brad dropped his bags on the great room floor and wrapped his arms around

Kate, kissing her with urgency. "Damn," Brad said pulling away slightly. "If we were alone I would seduce you right here, right now." The look in his eyes confirmed he would.

"Since we are not alone, you will have to settle for intelligent conversation at the moment," Kate said, regretting they could not follow through on Brad's desire.

"Can I at least talk dirty to you?"

"Only if you whisper in my ear." He did, and Kate blushed and socked him in the shoulder. "Stop that," she said, "or I'll turn that water gun on you. To change the subject, did you bring my data?"

"Yes," Brad said, "but you don't get it until I leave. While I'm here you have to listen to how difficult it was for me to get it and spend long mornings lingering in bed with me while we explore each other's bodies. I desperately need some down time and I suspect you do too. Besides, I have some troublesome news to share with you and Joe."

Joe and Shadow were making their way back down the stairs and Joe was giving him the standard cabin briefing that was becoming well rehearsed. "Nice tree," Shadow observed.

"Joe," Kate said, "Brad says he has some bad news for us. I'd rather get it over with than dwell on the possibilities." Everyone looked at Brad.

Brad sat on the sofa and looked at his hands before looking up and saying, "About three days ago, Robert was killed in the line of duty." Joe looked at the floor, exhaled loudly and shook his head.

Kate clutched her chest and sat down heavily in a chair, "That's terrible, what happened?"

"Unfortunately, or maybe fortunately in this instance, I can't share the details, but I can tell you it was an unpleasant situation and Robert handled it with courage."

"Poor Robert," Kate said putting her hands over her mouth and nose as she composed herself.

Joe was explaining to Shadow who Robert was and sharing some things he had done and said when he was at the cabin. "It's too bad he's not with us anymore," Joe added at the end of his story.

Kate got up and walked out to the arctic entryway leaving the cabin door open. Seconds later she returned and pulled one of the dining chairs over to the tree. She climbed up and extracted the Yankees stocking cap Robert had left behind from her pocket and placed it over the top of the tree. "I think we've solved our tree topper problem," she said.

"Good choice," Joe said and the others nodded their agreement.

"Everyone looks like they could use a drink. Scotch all around?" Brad asked. Everyone either nodded or murmured an affirmative. He came back with four drinks on a tray and passed them around before turning to the tree and raising his glass, "To Robert"

"To Robert," the group replied each raising their glasses to the tree before clinking them together and taking a sip. Kate wondered where the Scotch had come from.

The following morning, Kate woke to find Brad sitting on the edge of the bed watching her. He looked somewhat desolate. "What?" she asked with a nervous giggle.

"Nothing," he said forcing his expression from a frown to a smile, "I just like looking at you while you're sleeping. I miss you when I'm gone. No matter how far away I am I always want you to remember I care about you."

"Are you going somewhere?" Kate asked sounding slightly alarmed as she sat up in bed.

"No, I don't have any plans to go anywhere. I just realized today that you never know what the future holds. But enough of that," he crawled under the covers, "let's talk about the present. I am going to go downstairs and fix you breakfast in bed and then we are going to stay here for a while and experience and talk about happy things." As he said it, the buzzer announcing a satellite call sounded. "Shit, I think that's for me. I'll bring breakfast after the call." He got out of bed and ran for the communication room wearing only his boxers.

Thirty minutes later Brad arrived back in the bedroom with French toast, sausages, a carafe of cranberry juice, and a pot of tea. Kate didn't even know they had a carafe. "Shadow asked why *I* got to sleep with you. I told him it is because I am a privileged character and that he obviously has never tasted the power of my French toast," Brad chuckled. "Watch out for Shadow, he is plain spoken and is used to being the one with privilege, if you know what I mean." Kate just nodded; she was too busy eating French toast and thinking about where in the kitchen the carafe might have been.

Brad seemed to be going out of his way to make their time together special. They spent a great deal of time alone together in their room reading books and talking about politics, economics, and history, cuddling, and pondering life's pleasures and challenges. Though no one expected to exchange gifts for Christmas, Brad had brought Kate a diamond-shaped filigreed necklace made of white gold with five diamonds embedded in it and matching earrings. "These are beautiful," Kate said, "I just wish I had something for you."

"I already have what I want," he said kissing her forehead, "and shopping is not an option for you right now anyway. Although Joe did manage to convince someone at headquarters to order a sauerkraut-making crock for him and have it sent in with the supplies. I still don't know how he pulled that off, but we'll chalk it up to good tradecraft. How was the sauerkraut, by the way?"

"It was great," Kate said, "We ate it with brats, pork chops, and put it on Reuben sandwiches. I canned some too, if you'd like to try it."

"I think I might," Brad said.

Brad's plan was to stay until after New Year's, but three days before he planned to leave, he received a secure email message warning about an incoming blizzard and suggesting Brad leave early. They would also be sending in supplies two days ahead of schedule. Brad said he'd stay long enough to help them get the supplies in and then he'd head out. Kate and Brad picked the day before the supply run to take the snowmachines up to the foothills for lunch. As they sat on a sleeping bag Kate poured each of them a bowl of tomato soup from a thermos, unwrapped their tuna sandwiches, and opened their baggies of orange slices before shoving her hands quickly back into her gloves. "It's pretty cold out here," Kate said, "and the humidity has picked up too. I think there really is going to be a storm." She sipped some soup through the hole in her facemask and intermittently nibbled on her sandwich.

"It is so cold, that I am unwilling to make a pass at you out here," Brad said matter-of-factly.

"Mmmm, that's pretty cold."

"So tell me, what have you turned up in your research so far that requires the data you requested?" Brad asked.

Kate took a deep breath of the arctic air and coughed from the shock of it. "Well, it's complicated and perhaps not directly related to my research. I've finished decoding Max's program, and yes, I know Max wrote it."

"We don't think it's entirely Max's program, but we do think he was forced, against his will, to finish writing it," Brad said in a tone that implied he was no longer engaging in casual conversation, he was working.

"It appears to be some kind of master program designed to route orders through a variety of U. S. trading firms and financial markets," Kate explained. "It could be a program from a foreign exchange that is linked to U.S. markets, but the routing is unusual. Do you know where it originates?"

"We're working on it," Brad said mechanically.

"I want to use the data I asked you for to see if I can use stock routing information and other clues to track some orders back to the program to fully understand what it's doing operationally." She paused, but Brad had no reaction. Kate continued, "There is one thing that I really don't understand about it though. At the beginning of the program there is what appears to be some sort of input branch that contains an algorithm I don't understand. It looks like it's watching another computer program for information to make trading decisions on, but I don't know what. I think it's pulling data in from another program somewhere that's telling the program Brad worked on which trades to make. Any ideas?"

For a fraction of a second, Kate thought she saw Brad's eyes open a little wider, "Maybe," he said, "I'll check on it. I'm cold we should probably be getting back." Kate understood the conversation was over and that was okay with her, she didn't wish to tell him everything she suspected either.

The supply flight arrived the next day without incident and it was much easier to move supplies into the cabin with four people than two. Kate used the snowmachine to take Brad back to his vehicle in the parking lot and Shadow decided to ride along as well. Brad loaded up his things and then

returned to shake Shadow's hand firmly. "Thanks man," he said, "I appreciate everything you've done and are going to do."

"My pleasure," Shadow said, "I'm always glad to serve my country." They
gave each other a quick, manly, back-slapping hug.

Brad moved to Kate, put his hands on her shoulders, and paused to look
at her. "What is up with you, Boo?" Kate asked.

"You do realize that you are the only person on the entire planet I would
ever let get away with calling me Boo, don't you?" Kate smiled at him. "I'm
just learning to take a moment to appreciate you," Brad said before he hugged
and kissed her with a warmth and affection that surprised her. In the background she heard Shadow say, "Nice."

Brad drove off in the truck and Shadow and Kate rode back to the cabin
as the first few flakes of snow were starting to fall and the wind changed
directions.

CHAPTER 20

Late that evening the wind started blowing with a vengeance from the northwest. The weather station mounted on the corner of the deck showed thirty to thirty-five mile per hour sustained winds with gusts up to ninety miles per hour. If they were in Florida in August, this storm would have a name. Although the temperature had been in the single digits for days, the storm front was bringing the temperature up into the low twenties. Even though there was little snow falling at the moment, Kate knew these were the makings of a serious blizzard. The wind was already causing the snow on the ground to blow and drift dramatically and it sounded like the cabin windows were being pelted by pebbles. The roof creaked loudly and the entire cabin shuddered in the gusts. It was the first time Kate sensed the true isolation of their location. If something went wrong, there was no one coming to help them. They would have to, literally, weather the storm on their own.

Kate tried to sleep in her bed, but the sounds of the wind howling through the attic vents and the groan of the rafters made her uneasy. By one o'clock in the morning she grabbed her pillow and comforter and moved to the couch in front of the wood stove. When she arrived downstairs, she found Joe in a recliner watching television with the volume turned off and the captions on.

"Hi," he said, "I hope I didn't wake you, I was trying to be quiet."

"No, you didn't wake me. The wind is giving me some anxiety about the roof blowing off, so I thought I'd try to sleep on the couch."

"I couldn't relax enough to sleep myself. Shadow seems to be sleeping though," Joe said. "I don't think much bothers him, he appears to be remarkably in control of himself. I bet he's one of those guys who can change the rate of his heartbeat just by thinking about it. At this moment I both admire and hate him for that quality." Joe gave a nervous chuckle as something outside broke loose and was now banging forcefully on the side of the cabin.

They looked out the window and observed that the pole containing the cell phone range extender was bent near the roofline of the cabin and had broken about two-thirds of the way around the pole. What remained attached was beating against the cabin as it endeavored to break free. "One range extender's wind is another range extender's liberator," Kate said in a poor attempt to use humor to sooth the tension they were feeling.

"Do we need to go out and take care of that?" Joe asked.

"No," Kate said shaking her head, "There is no way to get a ladder up there right now, it would be too dangerous. It won't take it long to break free on it's own. Besides, it's snowing now too." The snow was coming down so fast and blowing so hard, Joe and Kate could not see the rail of the deck from the window. The varying speed and ferocity of the perpetual *bang, bang, bang* of the pole helped the pair judge wind speed and gusts since the weather station appeared to have departed the deck and was on its way to Japan or some other distant point. They should have written a note on it like the kids who attach letters to balloons to see where it eventually ended up.

"How long is this going to go on?" Joe asked hoping for an answer he could live with.

"This could last three or four days," Kate said. The look on Joe's face indicated that was not the answer he was looking for. As she said it, the television suddenly went out and nearly simultaneously the banging of the pole ceased. "Sounds like the pole is gone, but so is the satellite. It could be that the dish has been damaged or moved out of position, but it's more likely we can't get a signal through this storm. Hold on a minute."

Kate ran up the stairs to the communication room and checked the satellite phone. It was dead. She returned to Joe, "The satellite phone is out too, it's the storm. If the TV is out, we won't have internet either."

"Do you mind if I turn on the radio to mask the sound of this wind?" Joe asked. He looked somewhat rattled.

"Of course you may," Kate said calmly, as if nothing unusual were going on. If Joe panicked, she might panic and that wasn't an option. There was a slight hint of static, but the radio signal didn't seem to mind the storm much. Glenn Miller and his Orchestra were playing *In the Mood* and Joe grabbed Kate's hand and said, "Let's dance!" and they did until they were both so tired they were able to sleep with Kate on the couch and Joe in the recline. The radio continued its music in the background, drowning out some of the wind noise.

Early the next morning, Shadow came bounding down the stairs saying, "How about this storm?" waking Kate and Joe up from their short night's sleep. He looked disgustingly well rested.

"How did you manage to sleep?" Kate asked.

"Earplugs and a lot of practice sleeping in places with missile and artillery fire. I have more earplugs if you want them, they help a lot."

"I can't speak for Kate, but I will take you up on that offer tonight," Joe said.

Kate pulled open the blind on the window over the dining table to see what the weather was doing, not knowing how much she would be able to see since the sun wasn't up yet. As it turned out, she couldn't see much of anything because a snowdrift covered about two-thirds of the window. She climbed onto the table to look over the drift, but she couldn't see very far through the blowing snow. It did look like they were going to have to give up on trying to see the rail of the deck, since it was now buried under the drift. Kate would need to find a new focal point to judge visibility.

"I'm glad you find this storm invigorating Shadow, but we've lost our TV, Internet, and satellite phone, so I hope you enjoy board games," Kate said.

"I feel safer right here, right now than I've felt in a long time. Nothing like a storm to keep the bad guys away," Shadow said with a big, relaxed grin that reminded Kate of Harry Clark, without the Texas accent or the Padrón resting in his fingers. "If everyone is game I'd love to make us some omelets and biscuits with gravy for breakfast if you have the fixings. It's all I've been able to think about for the past two months."

"Sounds great, I'll get the coffee started," Joe said.

Shadow made flaky, homemade biscuits without looking at a recipe and the richest, most mouth-watering sausage gravy Kate had ever tasted. He also made spanakopita omelets with spinach, onion, and feta cheese. Kate was in heaven. "I want this meal every morning for the rest of my life," Kate said closing her eyes as she chewed her food."

"Glad you like it," Shadow said.

As they were cleaning up the morning weather and announcements came on the radio. There was only one announcement:

"To Out There Jane: We hear you're having a hell of a storm there and we're thinking about you. Tried to contact you through the usual channels, but no one was home to answer our calls. Can you get word out somehow to let us know if you're all right and if you need anything? Love Mom and Dad."

"Apparently we are not the only ones who have realized the satellite phone and Internet are out," Kate said drying her hands off with the dish towel, "I hope the shortwave antennae is still up and I can get ahold of the base that way. I'll be back." She headed upstairs to the communication room.

Kate turned on the shortwave radio, dialed in the band and keyed the mic a few times. It appeared to be working. She grabbed her code book and transmitted a series of numbers over the radio, "7-2-5-9-7…" The coded message said, "Eagle, this is Robin, do you read? Over." There was no answer so after a few moments she repeated the string of numbers. She received a response also in code.

"We read you Robin, how are you holding up? Over."

"Eagle, we've sustained some damage, all satellite is out due to weather, and we'll have to dig out once it's over, but we're secure. No immediate needs. Over."

"Glad to hear it Robin. Hang in there; it looks like it will be around for at least another 24 hours. Over."

"Roger that Eagle, we'll batten down the hatches. Over."

"Stay warm Robin. Over and out."

Kate went back downstairs to let everyone know she had made contact. "We have a problem," Joe said crooking his index finger to summon Kate to the kitchen. He turned on the faucet and only a few squirts of water came out. "Do you think it's frozen?" Joe asked.

"No, if it were frozen we wouldn't have had water earlier, the pressure tank is probably empty. I'd need to go out and start up the generator to run the pump and fill it. Dang it, I should have thought of this and had us conserving water," Kate said. "The next problem we're going to have is that the other generator is going to run out of gas and we'll lose our electricity."

"Do you think we can get to the power house?" Joe asked.

"Maybe." Kate went out into the arctic entryway and opened the outside door. Small tree branches and other debris appeared to have joined the swirling snow in the air and Kate lost her balance as a gust of wind blew snow, pine needles, and bark into the cabin. The wind appeared to be the least of her problems though because snow had drifted halfway up in front of the door and removing it would be impossible in the wind. She closed the door and looked out the side entryway window. What Kate saw appeared to be snow at least six feet deep as far as her eyes could see. There was no dark silhouette of the power house in the distance, it was buried under the snow. Kate reported back to the others and suggested it was time to bring up the emergency supplies and prepare for the power to go out. They did and about two hours later the generator depleted its fuel. Thank goodness they had a warm fire, a cabin built six feet off the ground, and Kate had remembered to bring the shovels inside the cabin.

The trio spent much of their time huddled around a couple of lanterns playing cards, games, and reading. Shadow taught them how to play Sheepshead, a somewhat complicated card game played with a deck of 32 cards from 7s to aces. The storm finally let up around noon the following day and they opened the door and starting shoveling their way out. They decided their first priority was to get to the power house, unbury it, and get the generators going. By 3:30, the sun was setting and they had only made it about two-thirds of the way to the power house, so they would have to go through one more night without power or running water.

It took the group three and a half days to shovel paths to everything, dig out buildings, clear the deck, and uncover the satellite dish. Spring, unfortunately, was still far away.

Chapter 21

Once the cabin was fully operational again, Kate returned to her work. She downloaded the U.S. market data on the fifteen specific and fifteen random stocks she had requested from Brad. Kate didn't know exactly what she was looking for, but knew the key would be in patterns of similarities and differences in order routing information and perhaps brokerages being used. Kate found that she wasn't able to stare at the files waiting for patterns to emerge for very long periods of time, so she broke it up into four work sessions a day. On her second day in the communications room, something unusual happened.

When she had made the shortwave radio broadcast during the snowstorm, she had inadvertently left the radio turned on. Since they were operating on a band no one else used, Kate didn't notice it was powered on because the radio stood silent due to lack of communication traffic. That day, while she was working, Kate heard the crackle and hiss of an open microphone that caused her to turn toward the radio. Then she heard a voice in a thick Eastern European accent say, "Dr. Adams, are you there? Can you hear me Dr. Adams?" Kate started as she reached over and turned off the radio. She knew it wasn't an official broadcast from the military base or another authorized communication center because they didn't use the established protocols. They also never used her name on the radio. Her best guess was that it was some new radio operator at the base goofing around as he was learning to use the equipment. After all, there was no reason for him to believe she would be listening and Eastern European accents were not uncommon in Alaska. She made a mental note to mention it to Brad when she saw him in a couple of weeks. She shrugged it off, there were more important things to worry about.

On the third session of the fourth day shortly after Kate had settled onto the stool, she noticed something. She ran a query on one of the fields to isolate the stocks that had a particular code. The results caused Kate's jaw to drop. All of the trades for the fifteen specific stocks Kate had picked contained a code that none of the randomly selected stocks did. The fifteen stocks Kate had requested were those that had had recent mini crashes in their prices. Her guess was that these trades were running through Max's program, but what was the purpose and where did it originate? *Max, code, program, trading, stock, markets, exchanges, routing, orders, traders. Traders, could it be...?*, Kate asked herself. Kate broke security protocol, picked up the satellite phone, and called MAK Software.

After the phone call, she opened a word document and started writing a paper on financial market security and the causes of mini-crashes. She still had a lot of unanswered questions, but based on her research so far and all the unsuccessful linear regressions she had run for correlations with different events in European Union stocks, she at least knew what didn't cause mini-crashes. Kate also knew this program did, but she just didn't know how or why yet.

Two days later at noon, the supply chopper arrived and dropped a large pallet onto an area in the yard they had cleared for it. The trio hauled the supplies into the cabin and Kate started opening boxes and moving things around inside them, looking for an envelope with her name on it. She found it in a box of paper goods. Kate pulled out the thick envelope, took it upstairs, and locked it inside the communication room before returning to help Joe and Shadow unload the supplies. "What was that?" Joe asked.

"That was the report from MAK Software that I need to read before our monthly conference call. One of the government projects they're working on is classified, so I'm required to lock it up," Kate said without missing a beat. She had planned for a question like that.

The three of them had lunch together and listened to the radio for a while, before Kate excused herself, "I need to go spend some time going through that MAK report before Tuesday's meeting and it looks like a thick packet. Even though I'm in the woods, I still have a business to run." She bounded up the stairs two at a time.

Kate turned on the desk lamp and held the padded envelope under it as she pulled the string though the brown paper to open it. She removed the accounting report she routinely received every month and set it aside. Next she reached in and pulled out a thick document that contained notes on Max's research on the orphan order problem he was trying to solve. The packet also contained any orphan orders in the past year for any of the fifteen mini-crash stocks Kate had selected. The stack of orphan orders for those stocks was two inches thick, double-sided, two hundred orders per page. "Holy shit," Kate said aloud when she saw it. She started counting the number of orphan orders that had the same routing code as the one's that appeared to run through Max's program. After counting up the orders on only twenty pages, Kate found the proportion of orders with that code to be around 98%. "I guess we'll call that a solid sample for now," Kate mumbled to herself. All of the orphan orders had one of two codes, the one in Max's program or one for what Kate guessed was a second similar program.

It appeared to Kate that someone was running a large number of orders through Max's program and then routing them through different brokers and exchanges. Two of the other routing codes used in the orphan orders matched the codes Max's program was using to identify the input points into different brokerages and exchanges. The reason these orders were "orphaned" and had no trader identification information on the order was because they were not being entered by traders at the brokerage, they were being inserted into the order stream just past the trader ID check. Kate wondered if Max knew about this malicious program the whole time and was only pretending not to understand the orphan order problem.

Kate now knew that someone was running a computer program to dump large numbers of buy and sell orders into the market by funneling them through legitimate brokerages so those trading firms looked like the originators of the orders. These large stock orders were causing instability in individual stock prices by causing mini-crashes and mini-spikes. By doing this they were increasing overall volatility in the market and making it look like markets were not functioning properly. This was worrisome to Kate, because when this happened in the European Union it led to regulatory restrictions on markets increasing to the point that the financial system in the EU had collapsed into crisis. Were they, whoever they were, trying to accomplish the same thing in the U.S.?

The other problem that remained was the mystery of the input program that seemed to be feeding some kind of information into Max's program to inform the algorithm about when, what, and how much to buy and sell. What was it and where was it coming from? It was time to have a serious conversation with Brad about what she knew.

Frustrated and angry, Kate decided it was time to walk away from the work until she had a chance to speak with Brad who could hopefully help clear some things up for her. She grabbed the MAK Software accounting report as she walked out the door. "The accounting report is not confidential," Kate said as she sat next to Joe on the sofa, "I can read it here, in front of the fire instead of in that freezing cold room. Where's Shadow?"

"He went out to start digging a path to the firewood so he can bring some more into the basement. We figure we'll be out in another week."

Suddenly Shadow exploded through the cabin door, leaving it open behind him. "We've got a drone," he said urgently as he ran up the stairs and came back with his sniper rifle case. "Kate, get the snowmachines running, you and Joe have got to bug out of here," he said as he assembled his rifle.

CHAPTER 22

"**W**hat do you mean, 'we've got a drone' how can you tell? Don't they fly miles in the sky out of sight? How do you know it's not ours?" Kate asked feeling like the only reasonable person in the room.

"Not that kind of drone," Shadow said, loading his rifle, "It's a small remote controlled drone. One of those quadcopters you see in hobby stores and it has a Go-Pro camera attached. It's looking for us and based on the remote control range on one of those things, whoever is flying it is within two miles and knows we're here. You have got to go, now! Get to your truck and head south toward Joint Base Elmendorf-Richardson." Shadow pushed her toward to door. "Joe, you'll need to go with Kate, but while she's getting the machines going, will you run upstairs and grab my bullet proof vest and the metal box of extra ammo under the bed? I'll cover the door." He moved the sofa aside, slid the ottoman to where the sofa had been, got down on his knees, rested his rifle and elbows on it, and sighted in the door.

Kate finally began to realize the gravity of the situation. She pulled on her outerwear and ran to the shed to start the snowmachines. She entered the shed through the side door and once she had the machines running worked to get the large double doors open so they could drive the machines out. "Shit!" Kate remembered the keys to her truck were hanging on a hook inside the cabin next to the door. She'd have to go back for them. She unlatched and pushed the large doors open and walked down the ramp, but then heard something that made her stop.

Snowmachines, quite a few, were bearing down on them from the East. She heard voices shouting above the whir of the machines, and caught flashes of movement between the trees; they were pulling onto the property. Kate ducked back into the shed, pulled the double doors closed behind her, and shut off the machines before they could silence theirs. She crept over to the side door and opened it a crack, just as the men jumped quickly off their machines. They left them running.

There were five machines with ten men dressed in matching white snowsuits and boots. They spread out around three sides of the cabin and six of them appeared ready to enter it. Four of the men crept up the front stairs while two stood at the base with their backs to the cabin to provide cover. Once up the stairs, the four men lined up two on each side of the front door. On the count of three, one man kicked in the door to the arctic entryway and then moved back to the side of the door with the others. Kate struggled to remember if she had closed the inside door as she waited for their next move.

Feeling more confident, the men went into the arctic entryway. Through the window Kate could see they had lined up, again two on each side, next to the inside door. The inside door must not have been closed because Kate never heard them kick it in. The next sound she heard were two shots from Shadow's rifle as the men presented themselves in the doorway, followed by a barrage of gunfire by the remaining two men. Glass shattered as the windows overlooking the mountain exploded out the rear of the cabin, followed by two more shots of Shadow's rifle, then silence. Six men remained.

The watchmen who had been standing at the base of the stairs were now on the deck, one on either side of the entryway door. One of the men on the ground yelled something to them and then climbed the stairs to the deck and crept around to the side of the cabin near the screened porch. They appeared to be speaking Russian, based on what she remembered from the language program that they had been studying that winter.

Another man joined the two near the door and they looked continuously at their watches. At what appeared to be an appointed time, the three men entered the cabin firing their weapons rapidly at the cabin's interior. There were two more shots of Shadow's rifle, but as the shots echoed, the man who had moved to the side of the cabin quickly and quietly entered through the side, screened porch door.

Through the cabin window Kate saw the man grab Shadow from behind and lift him to a standing position, kicking his rifle away as he did it. He placed his Glock against the base of Shadow's skull and in thickly accented English through gritted teeth asked, "Where is Dr. Adams? Tell me, or I will put a bullet in your brain." The rest of the men had entered the cabin and appeared to be searching it.

"I don't know any Dr. Adams," Shadow said calmly. "Perhaps you have the wrong cabin."

"You may not know her by that name, but Kate Adams has been living in this cabin. Where is she!" He pressed the gun harder against Shadow's skull, causing a nearly imperceptible wince to momentarily flash across his face.

"She's not here, I sent her away before you arrived. She has a good twenty-minute head start on you. She's headed north to Fort Wainwright in Fairbanks, if you leave now, maybe you can still catch her."

One of the men came down the stairs dragging Joe firmly by the arm. In English he said, "Girl not here, but found him. Should I kill?" He raised his Glock to Joe's temple.

"No, I have no matter to settle with him. However, this murderer has killed six of my best men." Without hesitation he shot Shadow in the back of the head, dropping him to the floor with a thud. Kate gasped and held her hand over her mouth so she wouldn't scream as she pulled back from the door and leaned against the wall. Once she had recovered control of her breathing, Kate mustered her strength and looked back out the crack in the door. Joe seemed to be alone in the cabin, staring in the direction of where Shadow's body must have been. He was weeping, his shoulders moving up and down as he did. She was certain Joe had no idea where Kate was and he probably optimistically believed Shadow was telling the truth and that she was already on her way to the military base. Kate hoped he would recover from the shock quickly and call for help.

The four remaining men had left the cabin and surrounded it on all sides. They were slowly walking outward in search of Kate. If Kate had a sniper rifle, and was a good shot, she could have hit three of them from her position. If she ever got out of this she was going to invest in one and the training to go with it.

Suddenly, the sound of electronic chimes pealed from Kate's coat pocket. Two of the men turned toward the shed door and Kate again pulled in against the wall as she fumbled to remove her mittens and retrieve the phone from her pocket to silence it. *Time to change the water filter,* read the reminder the phone had been clamoring about. Kate heard one of the men call out in Russian and discerned two men running, the snow squeaking like Styrofoam under their boots. Kate's breathing was controlled, but she could feel her heart pounding in her chest and the false strength of adrenalin pumping into her muscles.

She moved toward the far side of the shed near the double doors and unlatched the bolt. She reached up and unscrewed the light bulb. If she could keep it dark, she might have a chance. Her eyes were already adjusting to the dark, while the men outside would have to adjust from the harsh glare of the sun reflecting off the snow. It gave Kate an advantage, however slight. She quietly gathered a fire extinguisher, garden shovel, and tire iron around herself. She picked up a hatchet, raised it above her head, and waited as the man who seemed to be in charge said in a syrupy sweet voice, "Dr. Adams are you in there? We're coming in for you Dr. Adams." It was the same voice and mocking tone she had heard on the shortwave radio days before.

The men entered the side door single file and flipped on the light switch. When it didn't respond, the leader said something to one of the men in Russian and he ran out of the shed, presumably to look for a flashlight. The three remaining men walked slowly and carefully through the shed and stepped through the door of the workshop area and into the space where the snowmachines and ATVs were stored, near where Kate was hiding. She waited until the first two men had gone past her position and then leapt out and silently struck the hatchet into the last man's skull, which made a distinctive cracking sound as it landed. *That's for Shadow,* Kate thought as she picked up the tire iron and changed her position in the shed. The man let out a horrific scream before collapsing onto the floor of the shed. Blood trickled out around the edges of the hatchet and ran a short distance across the uneven floor where it congealed on the ice-cold concrete in a sticky pool. The others turned around and peppered where Kate had been with rifle fire. The sudden flashes of light momentarily knocked out Kate's night vision and she kicked a nearly empty paint can, sending it rolling loudly across the concrete floor.

The now third man returned with a flashlight and they started scanning the room with it as Kate got on her hands and knees to stay behind as many things as possible while changing position. She had worked her way back around the room and was crouched down next to the double doors. One of the three remaining men was blocking the doorway between the shop and the storage area, so she wouldn't be able to sneak out that way and get into the cabin as she had hoped. At least in the cabin she would have access to a gun and communications. Kate had stopped carrying her sidearm when the bears went into hibernation. Panic was starting to creep in and her breathing was getting harder and faster as the men continued searching the far side of the room. They would eventually find her; there was nowhere left to hide.

Kate was starting to have a difficult time controlling her adrenalin and with her fight options diminishing, her body was pushing her toward flight. As her panic reached the tipping point, Kate suddenly stood up, pushed through the double doors and started running toward the road. Kate knew it was absurd to think she could escape on foot, but, like people who jump from burning skyscrapers to avoid the flames and extend their lives by mere moments, Kate was extending her freedom and maybe her life for an additional distance, no matter how short.

The three men ran after Kate on foot and quickly overcame her. As two men held her arms, Kate tried to kick, scream, and bite her way to freedom as the third man rummaged through his pockets. A short time later she felt the bite of the needle in her neck, and she relaxed as her world faded to black.

Chapter 23

Brad burst through the control room door, "What the hell happened out there?" he yelled.

"Sir, we're still gathering information, but it looks like Shadow was killed and Kate has been kidnapped," a young woman sitting at a console explained calmly. "I'm trying to get surveillance in the air right now to see if we can track them. The snow might be helpful in that regard."

"Notify all the airfields in the area to be on the lookout for these guys, traveling with a woman. Contact the Canadian Border Patrol too, there's only two ways out of there, air or Canada. Where's Joe?"

"Still there. They let him live to tell the tale. Unfortunately he doesn't know much, he was pretty shook up after they shot Shadow and he thought Kate had gotten away. By the time he realized she was still on the property, it was too late for him to do much other than call us. He's beating himself up pretty badly about this. Says if he knew she was still there he would have armed himself and, I quote, 'started shooting the fuckers'."

"Who were they?"

"Joe said they spoke to each other in Russian and were wearing matching white snowsuits with arm patches on them. He said they appeared to be military style uniforms, but they seemed to be hired mercenaries rather than soldiers. With all their gear on they were pretty uniform in appearance, so he doesn't have any detailed descriptions, except that the leader had a pronounced five o'clock shadow. He's sending pictures of the bodies left on site right now."

"Hmmm," Brad, squinted at the pictures as they came up one at a time on the large screen at the front of the room. Shadow had shot every one of them in the face to avoid any bulletproof vests, making identification by sight impossible. "I can't tell anything from these. Anyone else see anything helpful?" No one answered in the affirmative. "Any word on how these Russian speakers found them?"

"All Joe said was that they sent in a small remote controlled drone with a camera just before they arrived on the property on snowmobiles, well he said snowmachines, but I think that's what they call them in Alaska."

"All right, I'm going out there to see what I can dig up," Brad said. "Get ahold of Rodriguez, Carr, and Ribali they're coming with me," Brad said to a gray-haired man in a crew cut with a roll of flesh creeping out over the top of his shirt collar. "Also, call in a cleanup crew; we're going to have to remove some bodies and blood from the place, but give me 24 hours there before you call them. And…I guess I'm going to have to bring the FBI in on this since a U.S. citizen was kidnapped and is being transported to who the hell knows where. I'll make that un-fucking-comfortable call myself. Shit, what have they done with her!" Brad yelled as he slammed his fist onto the console causing everyone in the room to turn and look at him. Suddenly self-conscious, Brad turned on his heel and stormed out of the room as the gray-haired man mouthed, *Wow*, to the person sitting next to him.

Two Anchorage-based FBI agents named Cotton and Suhler met Brad and his crew at the Anchorage airport. Brad was always somewhat suspicious of FBI agents in remote places like Alaska; he wondered what they'd done to get themselves stationed there. Cotton was the junior agent, a youngish 30 or so, who looked uncomfortable in a suit. Suhler was a woman in her mid to late forties with curly blond hair and a remarkably perky bottom for a woman her age. *She must be a runner,* Brad thought to himself just before, *I wonder if she's married?* Both FBI agents were carrying duffel bags. "We're required by policy to meet you at the airport in our suits, but if we're going where you say we're going, I think we'd like to change into more suitable attire," Suhler said with her voice rising at the end as if it were a question.

"Go ahead and get changed, we've got bags to pick up downstairs anyway," Brad said as he paused before heading to baggage claim so he could watch Suhler walk away.

"You're so obvious," Rodriguez scolded as she gave him a shove toward the escalator to baggage claim.

Suhler and Cotton arrived at baggage claim dressed more like people than bureaucrats and they were all loaded into a black FBI Suburban with government plates. Brad rolled his eyes when he saw it and longed for a nice CIA issued rental car that didn't scream: *Here comes the government!* They were towing a large enclosed trailer behind them.

The sextet arrived at the Amber Creek parking lot three and a half hours later and began unloading four snowmachines from the trailer. The two women, Rodriguez and Suhler, rode together and Cotton hopped on the back of Brad's machine, justifying it by saying he'd never driven one before. Brad resisted the temptation to tell him that Carr and Ribali hadn't either, but they were real men.

As they headed toward the cabin, it become apparent that whoever took Kate had come out from the cabin to the parking lot, but they hadn't gone in that way based on the tracks. When they pulled up to the cabin, Brad paused a moment to calm himself before throwing his leg off the machine. He led the group up the stairs and into the cabin, his legs feeling like lead weights.

The smell of Shadow's body had tainted the entire cabin. Shadow had fallen near the woodstove, the heat from which accelerated the decaying process. The shot out windows helped dissipate the smell somewhat. Brad guessed Joe had been in the cabin with the body so long that he didn't even smell it anymore. Joe stood up from the dining chair and Brad could immediately see he was struggling with the events he had witnessed. "Hey, Brad," he said, "I'm really sorry about how this turned out."

"You did everything you could," Brad said, putting his hand on Joe's shoulder.

The rest of the group had nodded to Joe, but walked past him and over to Shadow's body. Cotton grimaced and gagged when he saw the grotesque head wound and quickly looked away. Brad noticed, "Why don't y'all head outside and look around a bit before Cotton leaves his breakfast in here."

"Good idea," Joe said walking over to guide Cotton into the kitchen. By helping Cotton, he was helping himself. "Let's get you some 7-Up, the sugar will help with the shock and the soda will help settle your stomach. You can take it outside and get some fresh air, it'll help." Cotton took the can of soda, thanked Joe, and went outside with the others as instructed.

Brad and Joe walked over to where Shadow lay. Brad looked at him and sighed heavily before kicking Shadow's stiff, lifeless boot, "Dang it Shadow, why did you have to go and get yourself shot?" He was fighting back tears. It was Joe's turn to put his hand on Brad's shoulder.

After a few moments of silent reflection Joe spoke, "You two went way back, didn't you?"

"Yeah, Shadow had been at the Agency about a year before I came on-board and he was with me on my first field assignment. We hit it off right away and quickly became friends, bound by our mutual experiences. We always knew what the other one was thinking and it made us an effective team. My career eventually took me into the office, but I still relied on Shadow in the field."

"What was he doing here?" Joe asked.

"After Robert got picked up I just had a bad feeling. They had tortured him pretty badly and I didn't know what information he might have given up. While he didn't know the exact location of this safe house, he certainly could have told them its general location. Even though the people who grabbed Robert weren't the same people looking for Kate, you never know which bad guys are sharing information with which other bad guys. It probably got passed around in an intelligence exchange and eventually the people looking for Kate got wind of it and thought it was a lead worth following up on. I put a freeze on any new official guests and brought Shadow in to add some security, but the number of guys they brought surprised me. In hindsight I should have listened to my gut and just shut it down, but I didn't have any solid evidence either way." Brad's face was racked with grief.

"You've broken one of your own rules and grown very fond of Kate, haven't you?"

"I don't know exactly what I feel." Brad paused before changing the subject, "So tell me, as a psychologist, how did Kate seem in the days leading up to the event"

"Well, as you know when I called it in, she was onto something. I think she was starting to figure things out and at first it was a shock to her. Your visit helped settle her a bit, but she seemed to have an intensity I hadn't seen before and was getting very good at compartmentalizing her emotions and not showing her hand. If I didn't have some inside information about what she was doing up there, I don't think I would have thought anything was up."

"She's a tough bird, passionate and stubborn," Brad said.

"That she is," Joe nodded in agreement. "There is one unusual thing though. She received a very thick padded envelope with the last supply run. When I asked about it, she said it was the accounting report from MAK Software and that something they were working on was confidential so it needed to be locked up. I don't think it was just an accounting report."

"Well, let's see if we can find it." The documents were found inside the lockbox in the communication room. When Brad opened the envelope he found Max's reports on the orphan orders. "Shit, she's gone farther on her own than we thought she would. She knows too much, we've got to get her back."

Brad went outside and got Suhler, "We have to go see some neighbors," he said pulling her toward the snowmachine. They drove up the snow-covered trail until they came to the first mine that showed signs of snowmachine activity. They drove up to the miner's cabin. The smoke coming out of the chimney indicated he was there.

"Hold it right there," the miner said as he stepped out from the side of the cabin and gave Brad and Suhler an opportunity to look down the pristine barrel of his gun. They raised their hands in the 'don't shoot' position. "The only thing worse than a claim jumper is a government official from the IRS trying to steal your gold."

"Um...we're not from the IRS," Brad said with an unusual hint of nervousness in his voice, "Whatever gave you that idea?"

"You were with that woman, you came out here to check out my operation to see how much you could take me for," the miner said baring his teeth. They were tobacco stained and in need of repair.

"We're not from the IRS, I'm with the CIA and this is agent Suhler of the FBI. Show him your badge Suhler." She slowly reached into her pocket and handed her ID to the miner who studied it like the only thing that made sense to him was her picture as he kept looking at the photo and then back at Suhler.

"What does the FBI and the CIA want with me? Are you after that rogue IRS agent you were with too?"

"Who told you she was a rogue IRS agent?" Brad asked, dropping his hands.

"Them men who came by yesterday. They said she was an IRS agent that had gone bad and was here to find miners who hadn't paid their income taxes and then blackmail them for gold. Had her picture and everything, I recognized her right away. Worse than claim jumping I tell ya."

"Were these men wearing matching white snowsuits?"

"Sure were."

"Who did they tell you they were?"

"Said they were part of the IRS police and were here to arrest her. They wanted to know where she was stayin' so I told them I didn't know where exactly, but knew the area she was in. The only thing worse than the CIA and the FBI is the IRS, so what exactly is your business here anyway?"

"Those men were not the IRS police and Kate is not a rogue IRS agent. She is someone we were hiding from some very bad people and you gave her up. Believe me, the people you have turned her over to are ten times worse than the IRS, the CIA, the FBI, or any other alphabet soup agency that you find distasteful. Let's go Suhler," Brad was clearly angry as they turned to go.

Chapter 24

Kate slowly regained consciousness as a wave of nausea began washing over her; she started to gag. A woman with grey hair tucked under a light blue nylon kerchief said, "No, no, no," and turned Kate's head to the side and pulled her toward the edge of the bed where she offered a plastic bucket for Kate to relieve her nausea in. The nausea was replaced by a surge of soaking perspiration. The woman moved to a kitchenette along the opposite wall and made her a cold compress. The woman was overweight, probably in her 60s and was wearing a floral print dress with small overlapping yellow, pink, blue, and brown daisies, and sturdy lace-up shoes with a low heel. She looked like someone's grandmother or nanny, not a kidnapper.

The compress felt good on her head and the clarity of her surroundings was improving. They were on an airplane, a private jet to be exact, and Kate was laying on the lower of two bunks that folded out from the fuselage. They were airborne, based on the sound of the engines. Looking around made her nauseous again and she puffed out her cheeks and reached out as a signal that she needed the bucket. The woman responded appropriately. Kate hoped that was the end of it, but she doubted it. She lay back down and closed her eyes hoping it would help. Her vertigo continued, but at slower revolutions.

A short time later nanny kidnapper brought Kate a mug filled with chicken broth "Drink" she said, making the motions of someone drinking from a mug as she nodded her head with urgency. Kate sniffed the steaming liquid and decided she should probably force herself to drink some. She had no idea how long she'd been unconscious or when she last ate or drank. The salty broth tasted good and Kate swore she felt the first sip slide all the way to her stomach and slosh against the sides. She drank it all and would have taken more, but didn't want to push her luck.

The broth had stimulated Kate's bladder and she suddenly realized what her next immediate need was. She hoped she wouldn't have to use the bucket, but any port in a storm. Kate slowly sat on the edge of the bed and put her feet on the floor. The woman rushed over and said, "No, no. Stay," as she pushed Kate's shoulders in a way that indicated she wanted her to lie back down.

"I need to use the restroom," Kate said. The woman looked at her quizzically. *Great, she doesn't really speak English,* Kate thought. Had she been a man, pantomiming what she needed to do would have been less complicated. In an attempt to communicate her need, Kate stood part way up, pretended to pull her pants down, and then sat back down on the bunk as if on the toilet. The woman did not immediately understand. Kate did it a second time and the woman said, "Aaahhh," pointed a finger in the air and nodded her head to indicate she understood.

"Come, come," she said and took two steps toward the rear of the aircraft and waved for Kate to follow.

Standing was not easy and Kate failed on her first two attempts. Her legs felt numb and heavy and her head spun as she made and effort to stand. The woman offered to help her, Kate did not resist and the two of them shuffled arm-in-arm to the rear of the plane where the door to the lavatory stood open. Kate walked in under her own power hanging onto the safety rails installed next to the toilet. *So that's what those are for,* she thought as she heaved herself onto the blue-water filled toilet. While the toilet was standard airline issue, the lavatory was not. It took up the entire rear section of the plane and was embellished with green marble and gold plate. In addition to the toilet, it contained a sink with a gold-lined bowl and a small shower in the corner. Next to the shower, was a heated towel rack with plush, marigold-colored bath towels hanging from it.

When Kate finished, she pulled herself over to the sink and looked in the mirror. "Holy crap," she said quietly when she saw her reflection. Her hair was soaked from perspiration and starting to curl. A deep red and purple bruise had swollen her left cheek. There was a deep laceration over her right eye that someone had done a poor job trying to hold together with steri-strips. Her eyes were puffy and dark. It looked like she had been dropped on her face.

Kate carefully removed the steri-strips one at a time and stuck the end of each on the edge of the sink. She pulled open the wound to see how bad it looked and was impressed by its depth as she caught a glimpse of her skull. Kate turned on some warm water and used soap to try to clean the wound as best she could. There was a short cabinet that sat on the floor next to the sink, which Kate opened and found every toiletry imaginable, but no disinfectant. She patted the wound dry with one of the marigold towels and reapplied the steri-strips to better close the wound.

The woman knocked firmly on the door, "Come!" she said sternly. Kate opened the door and they made their way back to the bunk where the woman handed her another cup of broth. Kate nodded and said thank you, holding up the mug as she said it. The woman gave a sharp nod and turned away. Kate tried to ask the woman for some ice for her face, but communication was unsuccessful, Kate would just have to continue swelling.

About thirty minutes later, the door to the front half of the plane opened and a smirking man walked toward Kate as the woman scurried toward the lavatory. "Ah, I see you're awake," Kate recognized the timbre of his voice and its mocking note and identified him as the leader of the group that had kidnapped her, as well as the voice she had heard on the radio. He was about six feet tall and pleasantly muscled, with black hair that was either curly or had been badly ruffled by the rabbit fur ushanka hat he had been wearing earlier. His five o'clock shadow was now a fully developing beard and mustache. If he hadn't kidnapped her, Kate might have found him attractive.

"Why have you taken me? What do you want from me?" Kate shouted at the man.

"Money, my dear. I have taken you because someone has offered me a great deal of money to do so." The smirk returned to his face.

"Why? Why did they offer you money?"

He walked over to Kate and slapped her hard on her already swollen face. Kate screamed in pain as bursts of gold and red fireworks lit up her right eye before diminishing to sparkling flecks.

"It is not for you to ask questions! Remain silent and perhaps you will get to live a while longer."

The man walked to an overhead cabinet and pulled out a pair of nylon athletic pants and a sweatshirt and threw them at Kate, "Take a shower and put these on, you'll feel better. I'll have Ulyana change your sheets. Ulyana!" The woman scrambled back, they exchanged words in Russian, and Ulyana took Kate's arm and hustled her toward the lavatory.

After her shower, Ulyana sat with Kate at a small table where they silently ate a soup of pork, potatoes, and cabbage along with some dense, brown molasses bread. Kate refused the bacon grease offered to spread on the bread as well as the vodka. Ulyana was happy to consume Kate's share of both. With a full stomach, a clean body, and fresh sheets Kate fell asleep shortly after the meal. She awoke when the plane landed and looked hopefully at Ulyana, who just shook her head and said, "No," and signaled for Kate to go back to sleep. They took off again a short time later and Kate decided it was just a refueling stop and maybe a flight crew change. She wondered how long they had been flying.

After they took off the second time, Ulyana attached a handcuff to Kate's wrist and shackled her to a metal bar attached inside the bunk. She climbed clumsily up a collapsible ladder onto the top bunk and went to sleep, snoring loudly. Kate remained awake as the hours ticked by. She was getting hungry again.

CHAPTER 25

After what seemed to Kate to be the length of another three days, an alarm clock sounded and Ulyana groaned and stretched with enthusiasm. She was talking to herself in Russian and with a sigh and more words to herself, she carefully climbed down the ladder. Ulyana smoothed her clothes with the palms of her hands when she reached the ground and offered Kate a small, quick smile and a sharp nod before she made her way to the lavatory, still muttering to herself, but adding a wave of her hands in the air as she walked. The tenor of Ulyana's voice and the accompanying sighs and gestures impressed Kate as a *"How do I get myself into these situations"* type of monologue.

When Ulyana returned she untethered Kate and walked her to the lavatory. When Kate looked in the mirror, the swelling and bruising on her cheek had gotten worse, obscuring the vision in her right eye, and the cut appeared to be festering. As she left the lavatory she pointed to her laceration and tried to tell Ulyana she needed some disinfectant. Ulyana looked at the wound and seemed to understand. When they returned to the bunk she pulled a first-aid kit out of one of the cabinets. She squeezed a generous amount of liquid onto a cotton ball and began dabbing it on Kate's wound, Kate winced, but knew the burning meant the disinfectant was doing its job.

Ulyana made a breakfast of fried eggs, a grainy porridge, grapefruit juice, and coffee, which she took to the front of the plane before serving some to herself and Kate. After breakfast Ulyana started to pack things up, indicating their journey was about over. Kate was tired again, but forced herself to stay awake as she expected some sort of action soon. A voice came over the jet's speaker and Ulyana sat down in a seat and fastened her seatbelt. All the window shades had been closed throughout their journey, but now Ulyana opened the one closest to her and pressed her face to the window.

After they landed the bearded man came back to Kate's section of the airplane. He picked the handcuffs up off the counter and roughly bound Kate's wrists with them. He seemed to enjoy his position of power over a woman as he stroked Kate's shoulder with a mocking grin before kissing her on the cheek and placing a black cloth bag over her head. Ulyana spoke to him angrily and he responded with what Kate guessed was a stern invitation to shut her mouth. The bearded man pushed Kate forcefully to a seated position on the bunk as Kate heard the rattle of chains and heavy footsteps heading in her direction from the open airplane door. There was a new man on the plane and he bound Kate's feet with the shackles.

"Thank you for the cargo," shackle man said to the bearded man with an accent Kate couldn't quite place. "Your payment is here." Kate felt some type of a case brush her leg before each man grabbed one of her arms and lifted her off the bunk and onto her feet. They moved toward the front of the airplane. Kate found the shackles to be heavy and awkward causing her balance to be challenged and her movements slow. The men half dragged her to keep her going at their pace.

When they reached the door, Kate could smell the fresh air. It was hot outside, but not particularly humid. Kate could smell jet fuel and hear the whine of other small jet engines idling, taxiing, and taking off. "Stairs," the bearded man said.

At the bottom of the stairs Kate was placed into the back seat of a waiting vehicle. The seats felt like they were leather and it still had a new car smell even though the windows were open. Kate had to step up into the vehicle and had plenty of legroom so she assumed it was a large SUV. She heard bags being loaded in the back of the vehicle before the bearded man walked over to Kate's window and said, "It's been a pleasure Dr. Adams, good luck," as he slapped the palm of his hand on the roof and laughed as the vehicle drove away.

As they drove off, the windows were raised and the air-conditioning was turned to a level that only allowed her to hear fan noise. Kate started counting to herself, "one one-thousand, two one-thousand..." while creating a system using her fingers to help her keep track of the travel time. After about twenty-three minutes, the air-conditioning fan was turned down and Kate could hear more of her surroundings, but heard nothing except the sound of tires on pavement. About one hour into the journey they left the pavement and seemed to be driving on a gravel road. Kate could briefly detect a sandy smell before one of the men complained in English and the fan was adjusted to recirculate. The area they were in did not seem to be very densely populated and they did not appear to go through any cities or towns that Kate could detect.

There were three men in the vehicle and they spoke English to one another indicating it was their common language, but they spoke infrequently. The man in the backseat with Kate had a Russian accent and the two men in front had unusual accents Kate could not identify. At one point on the journey the two men in the front seat said, "Oooh no!" and the driver started honking his horn. The man in the passenger's seat in front of Kate rolled down the window and a horrible rotten smell that was a mix of wet dog, skunk, and garbage filled the vehicle. There was at least one animal outside the SUV and it made a short grunt that sounded like a strange mashup of a bear and a donkey. The passenger's seat kidnapper began yelling out the window in a language not familiar to Kate that sounded like a cross between Korean and Hungarian. *Where the hell am I?* Kate wondered as she continued counting.

As he rolled up his window and the vehicle accelerated, the man turned to the Russian accented man and said, "They always block the road with those animals, I can't stand it."

"It's terrible," Russian accent replied.

According to Kate's calculation they were driving in the vehicle for about two hours before they arrived in what sounded like a town or village. They drove through a market area where she could hear people barking their wares in the same language the man used when he yelled out the window. Kate was in his country. It was a crowded market and they moved slowly as waves of people flowed around the vehicle. Kate heard the bleating of sheep, the noise of the crowd, and could smell flat bread baking, cooking oil, citrus, and spiced lamb. Their single vehicle caravan passed, a dog barked, and no one seemed alarmed by a woman with a black cloth bag on her head.

They stopped somewhere well away from the bay of the market crowd and Kate was led from the cool vehicle into an oppressively hot building. Outside the air was hot, dry, and sunny and the ground she walked across was hard and dusty; dirt rising up around her like the Pigpen character in Peanuts cartoons. Kate coughed as she entered the building where it was sweltering, stuffy, humid, and smelled like rancid cooking oil and rotting vegetables.

She was led through the building until they stopped and Kate heard the reverberated clank of a large metal bolt lock and the creaky metallic sound of a door. As the men tugged on her arms for her to move forward Kate felt adhered in place, unable to move, so the men dragged her into the room. Once inside they removed her hood and Kate could see she was in a six by six foot room with a 60-watt incandescent light bulb incased in a metal cage hanging from the middle of the ceiling. The men had all donned ski masks before they took off her hood and other than their height, she couldn't differentiate between them. They didn't speak and it was too dark to see their eye color. There were wearing matching 'uniforms' of beige cargo pants and navy blue t-shirts. Kate's handcuffs were removed and she was shackled to a chain that was attached to the ceiling, her leg restraints were left in place. While she was standing, Kate was able to hold her hands near the front of her face with her elbows bent. The men left without a word and locked the metal door with a small barred opening, behind them. Kate looked around the room to assess her situation. In addition to the light bulb, there was a dead rodent hosting a swarm of flies in the far corner, assorted crawling insects, no exterior windows, and, Kate was starting to believe, diminishing air. The thickness of the building's stench made it difficult to breath and Kate was fighting a panic attack.

Kate heard another metal door open down the hall, then shouting followed by cries of pain, and the door closing again as a man sobbed. She was not the only one here. Exhaustion finally led Kate to slide her back down the wall and try to sit on the floor. When she did, Kate found that the chain was too short for her to get her bottom or knees onto the floor with her arms stretched overhead. The only way she would be able to sleep would be hanging from her arms.

Some time later two large men in ski masks opened the door to her cell and stood on either side. A petite woman in a Muslim headscarf entered carrying a paper cup full of water. *I must be in the Middle East,* Kate thought to herself, *and that animal I smelled and heard on the road was probably a camel, or more likely a caravan of camels to smell that badly.* But as the woman got close to Kate and handed her the water, she noticed something she didn't expect. The woman's flawless, pale skin and deep-set, hooded eyes implied she had Asian rather than Middle Eastern ancestry. Kate dismissed it as an anomaly. She demonstrated to the woman her difficulty with sitting down and asked if she could get a chair or something else to sit on. The woman just looked frightened by Kate's attempts to communicate and emphatically shook her head no and ran out of the room. *What are you thinking Kate? You're a prisoner, not a guest at a hotel.*

CHAPTER 26

Kate awoke to the sensation of searing pain in her shoulders and cramps in her neck. She had been unable to stay awake and fell asleep hanging from her arms with her head bent, chin resting on her chest. Unable to lift her head, Kate got her feet under herself to take the pressure off her arms. She was able to bring her right arm down under its own power, then had to use it to pull her immovable left arm back to her waist as a sharp pain coursed through it. Kate opened and closed her left hand as she tried to regain feeling as waves of shooting pain continued down her arm.

She reached up with her right arm and rubbed the back of her neck hoping she could get the muscles to stop their spasm long enough to push her head up. After a few minutes she was able to put the palm of her right hand on her forehead and push her head to the forward facing position. The relief made her groan. Kate guessed she had been in the cell for two days and her clothes were soaked with sweat and urine. She'd been given no food, only water brought by young women, all of whom appeared to be of Asian decent and practicing Muslims. The number of women made this fact no longer an anomaly. Kate was at a loss for ideas about where she might be, but she was quite certain it wasn't Alaska.

Today, the first woman who had brought her water arrived again only this time she was carrying both water and clean clothes exactly like the ones Kate was currently wearing. The men came in and unshackled Kate, then went out and closed the door. Kate rubbed her wrists and tested the range of motion of her arms. The right arm was stiff, but appeared to be all right; she couldn't lift her left arm beyond about forty-five degrees. The woman handed her the clothes, "No shower, clean clothes, yes?" Kate smiled and nodded, she was happy just to have clean clothes.

Kate used her right hand to slide off the pants and put on the new ones as her left arm dangled uselessly. Getting the sweatshirt changed was going to be a challenge. Kate leaned forward until her left hand could grab the cuff of the right sleeve and then pulled her right arm out before lifting the sweatshirt over her head and down her left arm. The reverse process got the new sweatshirt on.

The woman yelled something to the men and they opened the door and approached Kate. The tallest man walked behind her and pulled her wrists together behind her back. Kate yelled out in pain as she felt the ball of her left shoulder leave the socket before he snapped the handcuffs onto her wrists and placed the black bag back over her head. They dragged her back out of the building and roughly placed her into a waiting vehicle.

In the SUV Kate laid on the backseat and groaned loudly in agony. The driver kept yelling at her, but since she couldn't understand what he was saying, she didn't much care. Frustrated by her lack of compliance, the driver angrily pulled the vehicle over, got out, and opened Kate's door. He reached in, grabbed Kate by the back of her head and slammed her forehead into the center pillar, knocking her unconscious.

When Kate next woke she was in a room, two men were talking quietly in an adjacent room. Double glass doors were thrown open to a balcony, allowing a light breeze to rustle the chiffon curtains framing the opening. The air was fresh and clean, Kate breathed deeply to erase the memories residing on her olfactory receptors of her previous cell's decay. Her vision was blurred, but she was in a comfortable bed surrounded by soft cotton sheets and could see what looked like a room service menu on the nightstand to her left. *It must be a hotel*, she thought. Kate's headache was severe, but it served to make the stabbing pain in her shoulder seem dull by comparison. A door opened and then closed in the other room before the sound of men's dress shoes clipping across the floor moved in her direction. Kate randomly wondered if men still wore wingtips. She noticed her left arm was resting across her torso in a sling and she was wearing black silk pajamas with pink piping.

"Ah, someone's eyes are open," the man said cheerfully as he clapped his hands together. He was a tall, slim man wearing a light blue, summer-weight suit. The shoes she had heard were black, but not wingtips. His long, slim face was covered in neatly trimmed, gray facial hair, while the hair on his head showed signs that it was once dark. There were horn-rimmed glasses perched firmly on his nose. He seemed pleasant and good-natured with a breezy air about his movements that made it seem like gravity barely weighed on him. He sat on the edge of the bed.

"I'm sorry my colleagues didn't take very good care of you. I told them you were an important package, but to them your only importance was the money they would collect if they delivered you. Whether the contents of the package were damaged was irrelevant to them." His accent was light, but Eastern European, while his English had a British lilt. He smiled at her. "Next time I will change their incentives, but now let's talk about you. Your left shoulder had been dislocated, which my personal physician has reset for you, but there remains soft tissue damage that will most likely require surgery. For now it is in a sling and my physician has told me you will find it mostly useless in its current condition." Kate noticed the excruciating pain in her head was fading.

"You have a large welt on your head from trauma that left you unconscious, but no one seemed to be able to tell me how that happened." Kate, with great effort and care, touched her forehead and felt the painful welt. "My physician has given you two injections and prescribed some ongoing medication to help with pain and swelling in your head and shoulder as well as an antibiotic for the festering laceration over your eye. He cleaned the laceration and put in both internal and external stitches, it should heal nicely with only a thin scar. You may have a slight dent in the middle of your forehead from the trauma to your head. How exactly did that happen?" He seemed sincerely interested.

Kate licked her lips and tried to speak, but was only able to get an odd squawking sound to come out. "Hold on a minute," the man said running effortlessly into the other room and returning with a cold bottle of water.

"Drink this, it will help." Kate sipped the water and continued sipping until she could feel her throat slowly cracking open, allowing the water to flow freely.

"The driver didn't like my moaning so he smashed my head against the door pillar to make me stop. It worked." Her voice was just above a whisper.

"Well, that is unacceptable and I will address it. You are my guest now, so you don't have to worry about such things. I have ordered food, my physician said you would need to try to eat something as soon as possible. Rest until it gets here, I have some business to attend to." He got up and moved to the next room. Kate heard him dialing a phone before speaking angrily to someone. She dozed back off to sleep.

"The food has arrived, Dr. Adams," the man announced from the bedroom door. "My physician says it is best if you get up and move around a bit, he's worried about clots or some such. Here, I'll help you up." Kate suspected the man had probably learned his English in the UK or maybe South Africa when he was still quite young, based on his lilt and word choices. They slowly made their way to two chairs set around a room service table draped in a white linen cloth. The man started lifting metal covers off dishes to reveal warm pita bread, lamb shawarma with tahini sauce, tabbouleh salad, and a plate of vegetables that included cucumber, onion, tomato, cabbage, small dill pickles, and fresh mint leaves. The man spooned some tabbouleh onto his plate and picked up a pita, smeared it with tahini sauce, and began filling it with meat and vegetables. "Please eat Dr. Adams."

As they ate, Kate spoke, "You seem to have me at a disadvantage, you know my name, but I don't know yours."

"You may call me Archie, madam." Archie grasped the left lens of his glasses and repositioned them slightly higher on the bridge of his nose. His kindness made Kate uneasy and since she was learning to rely on her instincts as fact these days, she decided not to trust him. After all, he had paid to have her kidnapped. For now though, she was grateful for food, antibiotics, pain medications, and a bed.

During the next week Archie made little conversation and no demands except that she rest, take long baths, walk around the hotel's inner courtyard with him twice a day to regain her strength, and eat well. Kate did as she was told, she was too weak to resist if she wanted to. Instead, she focused on healing, observing as much as she could, and planning a possible escape once she had recovered somewhat. She peppered Archie with questions about who he was and why she was there, but his only response was, "All in good time, dear."

As long as Kate was willing to wear a headscarf and cover herself with a blanket, Archie allowed her sit in a lounge chair on the second-floor balcony. The hotel was near the market and large numbers of people flowed past, chatting, laughing, and enjoying their day. Now that Kate was able to see a larger cross-section of the population than she could from her former prison cell, she might have guessed they were in Indonesia or Malaysia, except the climate was arid instead of tropical and they were in a small town as opposed to a large urban area. She was running out of guesses and Archie refused to answer any questions about their location.

A strong majority, but not all of the population, appeared to be Muslim. Headscarves and modest dress seemed to be preferred over the burka, which was only worn by a small number of the women she saw. Women were allowed to walk around without a male relative and often came to the market in groups of 3 or 4 to shop and socialize with other clusters of women. There was a glass enclosed ATM across the street from the hotel that must have been for women only, but Kate couldn't read the sign to be sure. The enclosure was large enough for three women to squeeze in before they locked the door and conducted their transactions. Kate asked Archie about it.

"Ah yes, very observant. Women do not go into the bank, that is male territory, but they are allowed to use ATMs to get cash and deposit checks. The stand-alone machines are for women only."

CHAPTER 27

The next afternoon after lunch, Archie brought Kate a long, flowing black skirt, a bright yellow tunic-style top with flowers embroidered around the neckline, black lace-up boots, and a red headscarf with yellow flowers. "Get dressed, we have an appointment," Archie said cheerlessly. *Here it comes*, Kate thought, finally she would find out why she had been brought here.

Kate emerged from the bedroom in her new clothes and her sling to find Archie standing with car keys in his hand. "It won't be necessary to restrain you, will it?" he asked more as a statement than a question.

"Of course not," Kate said forcing as sweet a smile as she could muster under the conditions. She was pleased to see that playing nice had helped her gain Archie's trust somewhat. Perhaps it would eventually provide her with an opportunity to escape.

They walked down a set of service stairs in the rear of the hotel and out a back door into an alleyway where a white four-door Mercedes was waiting. Archie opened the back door for Kate and she got in. "You will forgive me, won't you," Archie asked showing Kate the black cloth bag he was about to put over her head.

"If you must," Kate responded, grateful not to be bound.

They drove for about an hour before Archie shut off the car. He ran back to open Kate's door and remove her blinder, "We have arrived."

Kate stepped out of the car and opened her mouth in surprise before she felt the first wave of laughter work its way up from her belly. She doubled over as she laughed while Archie watched in dismay. He had taken her into a desert area with course, rocky sand, not the fine, drifting sand that creates massive dunes that you see in movies. Poking up from the flat, lifeless desert were three wooden platforms topped with temporary canvas yurts, forming a triangle about twenty yards away.

"Ask for a yurt in a remote place so you can find yourself, and this is what you get", Kate said as she choked with laughter, "Except I can't even find myself on the map right now." More laughter as tears of amusement, frustration, and possibly madness ran down her cheeks.

"Dr. Adams, I would recommend some decorum, the man we are going to see will not find this amusing. Have you gone mad?" Archie asked as he tugged Kate's good arm toward the yurt to their left. Kate tugged it back so she could wipe the tears off her face as her laughter wound down to a spastic chuckle.

The wooden door that had been installed in the canvas structure opened as they approached and Archie insisted Kate enter first. A man who looked almost identical to Archie, except younger, stood waiting in the center of the round room. He stretched out his hand, "Ah, Dr. Adams, it is very nice to finally meet you. I'm Archie's brother Phillip." Kate stood silently and without expression. She didn't shake his hand. *Be calm,* she told herself.

"Why don't we have a seat," Phillip offered motioning to a grouping of four high-backed, gilded armchairs set around an oval coffee table in the middle of the room. As they sat, a man wearing a Sikh turban placed a silver tea service on the table before filling three cups from the teapot. He handed Kate a cup and saucer and she turned to him, smiled, and offered a nod of thanks. The man returned her nod, added a smile, and offered cream and sugar, which Kate refused. As he handed tea to Archie and then Phillip, they acted as if the man wasn't in the room, until Phillip dismissed him with a wave of his hand.

Kate sipped the dark, black tea, which was bitter and smoky as if tobacco leaves had been steeping in the pot. Phillip reached out to take a dried apricot and a couple of almonds off a plate on the tray. He looked toward the ceiling and closed his eyes as he chewed the fruit and almonds. When he finished he looked at Kate and grinned, "We enjoyed having your husband in our company for the brief time he was with us. He was a smart man who loved you very much. It was his love for you and his concern for your safety and well being that led him to see that helping us was his best option. We are hoping you have as much interest in your safety as he did and will come to a similar conclusion." Phillip said arrogantly as he formed a tepee with his hands and began tapping his fingers together lightly.

"We suspected your husband was a threat to us in Singapore when he began asking questions during visits to exchanges and trading firms about whether they had experienced problems with orphan orders and what they were doing about it. Since he was studying the problem so deeply, it was only a matter of time before he began to suspect what was causing it, in fact he already had some suspicions. However, *we* suspect you know more than he did. We have heard your speeches about the risks of foreign governments interfering in financial markets, even weaponizing them to manipulate currency and stock market values. What do you know about such things?"

Kate sipped her tea and looked at Phillip quizzically, "I only know that Max was trying to figure out what was causing the orphan orders. I'm a professor, not a programmer, I don't understand his work." She refrained from batting her eyelashes to punctuate her false innocence. She didn't wish to over sell it.

Phillip chuckled, "Oh, please Dr. Adams, we know better than that. You're an intelligent woman. You've worked with your husband on financial system development, you understand the intricacies of financial market structure, and you've been hidden away in the middle of the wilderness by the government. You cannot expect me to believe you know nothing about what is going on!"

"I certainly don't understand what's going on, including what exactly it is that you want from me. I assume you didn't bring me here to consult on the orphan order problem anyway."

"Of course not, we want to know what you know and who you have told so we can start modifying our processes to ensure they are undetectable. Second, we want your help with, shall we say, moving our plan forward." Kate sat silently looking at Phillip as her left shoulder throbbed, she wiggled her fingers to encourage circulation. Phillip smirked, "Of course if you don't agree to work with us, we will return you to the gentlemen we picked you up from and they can work on getting the information we need, or kill you should it become necessary. It's up to you. We'll let you think about your situation overnight and we'll talk again in the morning." He looked at Archie, "You may take her away now."

Archie stood and moved toward Kate. Kate held up her hand in a 'stop' gesture before finishing the last two sips of her tea and popping a dried apricot into her mouth. She stood up on her own and bowed slightly to Phillip, "Thank you for your hospitality." She managed to say without the sarcasm she heard in her head. When Archie grabbed her arm, Kate pulled it back, if she was going to die, she was going to face it with dignity and grace. She would not be dragged to it.

Archie led Kate to another yurt divided in two by a canvas panel. Each side contained the equivalent of a bedroom. "This is where Phillip and I sleep, you'll sleep on the other side." He pointed toward the smaller sectioned room with a single cot, a small bookshelf with a fan spinning atop it, a folding chair, and a large water pitcher and washbasin. "Don't even think about running, there is nowhere to go. We are well off the main road and there is nothing but dessert as far as you can walk. I will come and get you for dinner." He turned abruptly and left, obviously irritated.

Kate could hear a generator running nearby. She looked through the hole in the canvas that served as a window and saw it chugging away next to the third yurt. Near it sat a portable satellite dish. Kate crept out of the yurt and quietly made her way toward the third yurt. As she did, Kate could hear a loud, spirited discussion coming from the canvas structure where Archie and Phillip were. Once she made her way to her destination, Kate peeked in through a window that was covered in mosquito netting. She saw three men wearing black jackets facing each other, sitting at tables arranged in a triangle in the center of the room. They each had two computer screens in front of them and were typing away on their keyboards.

Behind each man was a rack of servers and other computer equipment. A small portable air-conditioner hummed in the far corner of the room and

Kate could feel the cooled air of the tent against her face. She wondered if this was where Max had been forced to work as he complied with the men's requests in order to keep them from harming her.

Watching the men work provided no additional clues as to what they were doing, so Kate returned to her sleeping quarters where she found a book on the sparsely populated shelf about the history of global currencies and settled into the folding chair to read it. She had accepted her fate, but was grateful for Max's courage. Despite his best efforts, he was ultimately going to be unable to save her. Death was going to come to her here; Kate just wished she knew where 'here' was.

At dusk, Archie arrived to announce dinner was ready. Kate looked at him wearily, "I think I would prefer to eat here. Perhaps your man could bring me a tray."

"Perhaps you will get no dinner at all if you do not come with me!"

"Well," Kate smirked, "A weak and hungry Kate does you no good, now does it?" She needed to take back some control from these men, she was tired of being submissive in hopes of saving herself. They had taken her to the brink of nothing to lose. Archie turned on his heel and marched out of the tent muttering angrily to himself. Thirty minutes later, a tray of food arrived carried by the man in the turban, who looked amused.

Kate slept well that night for the first time since she had been kidnapped, acceptance had brought her peace and courage. In the morning after she had finished the breakfast that was brought to her, Phillip entered. "It seems my brother lacks the stomach for our business sometimes, so I've decided to speak with you alone to convince you to see things my way."

Kate looked at him blankly, "You still haven't told me exactly what you want from me other than an accounting of what I know, which is little."

Phillip chortled, "Dr. Adams, your prattle amuses me, but I can make rather accurate assumptions about your knowledge, so let's move on to other business. Let's assume you know that our goal in the U.S., like it was in Europe, is to disrupt markets so that it looks like there is something wrong that requires intervention or gives cause to abandon markets due to their instability. We are essentially trading salvos by using the trading of securities as a barrage of bullets against the U.S. Of course in Europe they helped the process along by piling oppressive regulation onto financial markets once they appeared unstable, actually causing them to become even more inefficient than we hoped. We couldn't have asked for a better result. Our long-term goal is to move the major capital markets away from the U.S. and Europe, to our spheres of influence within Russia, China, India, Brazil, and Singapore.

We have already been quite successful in the U.S. with our propaganda campaign. It's easy to get the U.S. proletariat on your side when they don't have jobs, the stock market is climbing, and the government is spending on war instead of feeding its people. They applaud those who wish to destroy financial markets and the capitalist class they blame for their plight. Of course, it is the very global power of capitalism that we wish to steal from you and harness for our ourselves and our countrymen." Philip looked pleased with himself. He relished his role as the master manipulator who would bring down the U.S. financial system—as he had done in Europe—with the cooperation of its citizens. Assuming the outcome was inevitable, he was in no hurry. All he had to do was wait for the fall and capital would come rushing into markets within his influence. Kate feared he might be right.

"So what is it exactly that you want from me? It sounds like you already have this all figured out." Kate glared at Philip to convey her disapproval. As she asked, one of the men she had seen yesterday in the computer tent arrived and signaled that he needed to speak with Philip. Philip excused himself and walked out, leaving Kate to her own thoughts for nearly twenty minutes.

"I am sorry about that, apparently we are having some difficulties with our input program that gathers and processes the data that informs us on how to make our disruptive trading decisions, but I don't need to explain that to you, you are probably already familiar with it."

The input program was the only piece missing from Kate's puzzle. She had seen that there was some sort of program that fed information into the processing program Max had been forced to work on, but had no idea what it was or what it did. "I'm not familiar with the input program, what is it?" Kate leaned forward in her chair in anticipation as she asked.

"Ah, I can see from your enthusiasm that you do not know about the input program. Well, that pretty much sums up my inquiry about what you do and do not know. That was painless now, wasn't it?" Philip sat back in his chair, folded his arms across his chest, and grinned with satisfaction. "You can make the rest just as easy on yourself. You don't have a choice, really."

Kate's cheeks flared red as she became aware of her mistake. She had relinquished some of her control and needed to regain it. "I have never been in a situation where I did not have a choice. Sometimes, both choices lead to undesirable outcomes, but I always have a choice." Kate squared her jaw and waited, focused on her breathing...*deep breaths...in through the nose, out through the mouth.*...

"All right Dr. Adams, let me lay out your choices for you," Philip's nostrils flared as he said it. "Your company, MAK Software, worked with many different Wall Street firms and exchanges to try to solve the problem of orders flowing through their systems absent a trader ID number. The orphan orders your Max called them.

I know when your programmers were working with these companies they were given lists of the valid ID numbers individual traders use. While I have been able to get people inside firms to steal trading programs and algorithms for me to insert into my master program, I have been unable to get lists, by company, of valid trader ID numbers. While this may seem like it should be a simple hack, it has not been the case. They are only visible on the order when they are entered and when they return as confirmed orders otherwise they are masked. When ID numbers are entered on the order entry screen, they show up as dots just like when you enter a password, so even if I can mirror a machine when the order is entered, I can't read the number. All the trader ID lists inside companies are encrypted and the only ones who know the ID number are the individual trader and the computer and we have been unable to break the code on the server encryption. Silly, isn't it? After all we have been able to do, we can't get a simple ID number.

We've been able to place orders into their systems by inserting them just beyond the ID check that happens when the order is entered, but the lack of ID number is drawing attention to our activities and making us vulnerable. I want you to give us the list of the firms' decoded ID numbers. With that information and some clever hacking, we should be able to break their code. If you choose not to help us, we'll kill you. Those are your choices."

Kate knew that once he got the information he wanted, Philip would have her killed anyway. The outcome for her would be the same no matter what she did, but she didn't intend to die knowing she had given away the key to the continued destruction of U.S. markets. "Kill me," Kate said with conviction, taking control of the situation once more.

"It won't be quite that easy for you. I'm going to give you three days to think about it in your former cell, perhaps my colleagues will help you change you mind."

Three hours later Kate found herself once again surrounded by the smell of rot as she was thrown into the same cell. Outside her cell Kate could hear Philip giving another man instructions.

"Give her three days of...persuasion. If you can convince her to cooperate with me you'll be well rewarded. If you can't...kill her and dispose of the body, same as the last one." They hadn't bothered to chain her this time, but Philip took her sling away. "I would hate for you to hang yourself before we have finished our business," Phillip sneered as he walked away.

As Kate looked around her now familiar cell, she noticed that in the corner of the room maggots wiggling out of the dead rodent's decomposing carcass had replaced the swarm of flies from her previous visit. The collection of other insects appeared to be the same. A large cockroach made clicking sounds as it scurried across the concrete floor. Kate sat with her knees pulled to her chest in the opposite corner and prayed death would come easily and quickly. She was ready. She thought about Max and was comforted by the hope that the next life would allow her to be with him again.

Thoughts of Brad and what he must be going through entered her mind, Kate remembered well the stress, anxiety, fear, and uncertainty she felt when

Max disappeared and regretted that she was putting Brad through the same thing. It would be yet another burden he would have to overcome if he was ever going to have a real relationship ever again. The weight of what she was about to endure exhausted Kate and she dozed off with her head resting on her knees.

CHAPTER 28

The clank of the door opening woke Kate just as the man with the five o'clock shadow walked into the cell. Two armed guards from the holding facility stood in the cell on either side of the door. The bearded man squatted down in front of Kate. "I heard you were back," he was smirking as he always did. "I was passing through and thought I would stop in to see you. I'm guessing you were a bad girl and didn't cooperate." He stroked her cheek. "A few days here without food or water might help you change your mind. I'm just sorry I can't stay and help them convince you." He leaned forward and kissed Kate hard on the lips as she grimaced. "Such a waste," he turned and walked out the door. One of the guards left with him, but the other guard hesitated, staring at Kate intensely before he left, locking the door behind him.

There was a lot of activity in the building. People in other cells were belligerently shouting at guards, guards were yelling back, and many detainees were coming and going over short periods of time. There was always noise. The facility seemed to be a transfer site to traffic people from one place to another. There was no indication that any long-term imprisonment, torture, interrogation, or other 'services' were regularly being offered. It consisted of a single, relatively small rectangular building with cells running along the back and living quarters in the front. The men running it appeared to be locals simply operating a transfer point for profit. The guards were all young men, overseen by two older gentlemen who were most likely the owners.

The entire operation struck Kate as amateur, the professionals were the ones dropping off and picking up.

As the hours and days passed, Kate dozed, but was unable to sleep. Hunger and thirst were making her uncomfortable and weak in the sweltering room. The skin on her arms felt like it was shrinking and shriveling, and she frequently smelled smoke that wasn't there. Time disorientation had been a problem ever since she left Alaska, but she had now given up trying to figure out what time it was or how long she had been there. Death was her next destination and she needed to keep marching toward it until she got there.

The building seemed quieter now and there was less activity. Was it nighttime? Which night? It seemed like a long time since she had seen anyone, she tried to cry, but was too dehydrated to produce tears.

Kate thought she could hear the metallic scratching of the bolt on the door before the door opened slowly with a low groan. *Maybe today is the day,* she thought. The guard who had stared at Kate so intently the last time he was there came in and closed the door, but did not latch it. He swaggered over to Kate and looked down at her in a way that made her blood run cold. He wasn't here to kill her. She sat up and pressed herself into the corner. *Oh no you don't,* she thought, *you are going to regret this.*

The guard lightly touched her breast and Kate slapped his hand away. He laughed lightly, amused and excited by her resistance as he unzipped his pants. Moving closer to her he removed himself from his pants and grabbed Kate's breast again, this time firmly as he maneuvered his penis toward her mouth. With renewed strength Kate moved forward, mouth open, and looked up at the guard and smiled. He was pleased with her response until she placed him in her mouth and bit down as hard as she could.

The man howled from the bite as Kate grabbed his testicles, squeezed with all her remaining strength and gave them a firm twist causing the pitch of the howl to move into the upper register. *Nice range,* Kate thought to herself snarkily as he repeatedly hit her in the face trying to get her to release him. But Kate had become numb, she held firm. Three guards and one of the men in charge ran into the room and grabbed Kate. She let go. The guard clutched himself and continued wailing as the other guards helped him out of the room, blood trailing behind him. The man in charge stayed behind briefly, looked at Kate's bloody mouth, and spit on her as he turned to leave.

Basic animal instincts had awakened in Kate and she had found herself trying to suck as much of his blood as she could to quench her thirst. She would not go gently. When it was over, she wiped her face and moved to the far corner of the room where she began picking the maggots off the rodent carcass and swallowed them whole. She slept.

What she assumed was the next morning, one of the women she had seen before arrived in the cell carrying some folded black cloth. "You cannot let the men see you. Must put on. I help" She handed what she was carrying to Kate, she unfolded it to find it was a burka. Kate shook her head and hoped this piece of fabric had some magical power to repel men. She'd rather have had a cloak of invisibility. With the help of the woman, she put it on. It seemed like fitting attire, she could die directly inside her own body bag.

Not much later, Philip arrived in the cell. Kate had been sleeping and when she awoke she found herself covered in spiders, which she immediately and desperately, tried to brush off without much success. "You are a handful, aren't you? I hear you created a little excitement around here. Nice burka by the way." He laughed at her. " I can take you away from those spiders if you are ready to help me."

Suddenly aware of what she was doing, Kate stopped thrashing, set her jaw and sat still as, out of the corner of her eye, she watched a spider crawling across her cheek underneath the burka. It was getting closer and closer to her mouth. As the spider reached the corner of her mouth she looked directly at Philip and said, "Fuck you," and stuck her tongue out, grabbed the spider with it, and pulled it into her mouth. She glared at Philip as she chewed and swallowed.

"Well, you are a piece of work, aren't you? As they say in the movies, I'll see you in hell." He called in one of the owners. "She's all yours, dispose of her." Kate was left alone in the cell. *At least it ends today.* She lay down with the spiders and went back to sleep.

"Get up!" It was the owner and two guards and they were pulling Kate up off the floor. He said something to the guards and they began beating the bugs off her burka. Walking was impossible for Kate, so they dragged her to a waiting van where they roughly threw her onto a mattress in the back. To Kate, the bare, musty mattress was like an upgrade to the Presidential Suite at the Hilton, but she could still feel the sting of the abrasions and bug bites on her arms and legs. She fell back to sleep as she waited for death.

The noise of a helicopter woke her. *The supplies must be here,* Kate thought as she struggled to regain consciousness. *Why can't I get up? I wonder if Joe knows the chopper is here. Where's the sled? I wonder if the bananas are frozen again?* Kate was struggling to open her eyes and while she could hear the sounds of the helicopter, she couldn't figure out where she was.

Suddenly the doors opened in the rear of the van, light and blowing dirt enveloped Kate as she was pulled onto the ground. "You have to walk!" the man shouted over the noise. He kept lifting Kate up and setting her down, kicking at her feet until they were under her. Kate staggered along. In front of them was a helicopter with four men holding military style rifles, their heads rapped in cloth turbans, bandanas covered their faces leaving only their eyes exposed. The men were standing about six feet out from the chopper's open side door, They were fit and wore beige cargo pants, black boots, long-sleeved black t-shirts, and a nervous demeanor. Kate's captors seemed agitated as well. The groups were now about ten feet apart and looking at each other, unsure what to do next.

One of the men near the helicopter reached up and touched his right ear as if he was trying to listen to something through an earpiece. He shouted across, "You need to take the burka off her!"

"No, no, the whore goes as she is! We do not want to look at her!"

"You need to take it off! We can't tell if it's the woman we're looking for or if you've strapped any explosives to her!"

"It is the one and she has no bomb! Look!" The man took the butt of his rifle and struck Kate hard in the right ribcage causing her to slump onto the dirt. "If she had bomb, she go boom!" Kate lay on the ground gasping for air and coughing up blood. No one moved.

Kate struggled to lift her head and looked toward the helicopter. When she did, she could see a man inside the chopper leaning part way out the door holding a duffle bag. The crinkle of his eyes, his physique, and his controlled demeanor led Kate to believe it was Brad. How could she let him know they had the right woman? Kate coughed hard before saying as loud as she could, "Skeeter, it's me!"

"Grab her let's go!" Brad said throwing the duffle out the door, onto the ground. The four men grabbed Kate and carried her quickly, but gently, into the helicopter. It took off as soon as the last boot cleared the ground.

"It hurts!" Kate gasped as she coughed up more blood.

"It's okay, you're safe now," Brad said soothingly as he held her hand and stroked her hair. A medic had placed an oxygen mask on her face and was starting an IV. He told her she'd have relief from the pain soon. Kate lost consciousness before the medicine reached her bloodstream.

Chapter 29

Beep, beep, beep. Dr. Swanson, room 215. She should be coming out of it soon. I'll bring you a pillow and blanket. Try to get some rest. Have you eaten? Shwish, shwish. Click. Come on Kate. Squeak. Rumble, RUMBLE, Rumble, rumble.... Hey, how's she doing?

Kate was becoming aware of the sounds around her, but she still felt so tired. She tried to open her eyes. They fluttered. She felt a hand on hers and a heard a voice, "Hey Kate, are you waking up?" It was Brad. She tried again and managed to open her eyes halfway, but couldn't focus. Suddenly a bolt of panic struck her and Kate gasped as she tried to sit up and flee, but the pain was excruciating. She managed to move about an inch before she had to lie back down.

"Easy Kate, you're safe, you don't have to go anywhere. How are you feeling? Are you in pain?" Brad was stroking her hair.

Kate could feel her breathing was labored and her lungs hurt. "Yes," she said with remarkable clarity, "Where am I?"

Brad reached over Kate and hit the call button on her bedside controller. "You're in the hospital, on a military base in Germany."

"How may I help you?" the voice on the controller speaker interrupted.

"Yes, Dr. Adams is awake and in some discomfort. May she have her pain shot?"

"Of course, I'll be right there."

Brad returned his full attention to Kate, "We evacuated you to a military field hospital in Afghanistan where they stabilized you. You had surgery there to repair a punctured right lung and four broken ribs. You were also badly dehydrated and had a rather serious bacterial infection both of which they were able to get under control before we brought you here. You also have a torn labrum and rotator cuff in your left shoulder that will require surgery when you've recovered from your lung and rib damage. It also appears that you suffered a concussion at some point and since we didn't know anything about how the injury happened, we've been treating it as a traumatic brain injury, which means we've kept you in a drug induced coma for a couple of weeks to manage any potential swelling on the brain."

"I cannot tell you how weary I am of waking up in strange places and getting my medical report," Kate said dryly. "Who were those men and how did they find me? Where was I when you picked me up? What language was everyone speaking?" With her returning clarity of mind she found that all of her unanswered questions were also returning.

A male nurse in military fatigues arrived to press a syringe full of medication into Kate's IV tube before Brad could answer. This time she remained conscious long enough to enjoy its relief and as Kate relaxed she suddenly felt it urgent to tell Brad what she knew. Kate explained in detail how Archie and Phillip were involved in a plot to disrupt U.S. markets, like they had in Europe, in order to get capital to move offshore to countries within their sphere of influence. "Their plan is not to trigger a major market event like a crash, but to create a series of smaller, anomalous events that no one can fully explain in order to cause people to lose faith in U.S. markets. They are rigging the markets to make them look untrustworthy and unreliable." Brad's expression remained unchanged. Kate squinted at him and frowned, "But it seems like you already knew that, didn't you."

Brad looked at his hands as he rubbed them together, "To answer your initial set of questions, you were in the Xinjiang Uyghur Autonomous Region in northwestern China. It's the Muslim region of China and shares a small border with Russia. With this war being waged around the world, the Chinese government was concerned about uprisings in the region, but worried about global sentiment if they were forced to fight or otherwise oppress their own people. To solve this problem, about five years ago the Chinese allowed the

Russians into the region to contain the Muslim population. The Russians have started to use the region as kind of a large Guantanamo Bay and employ many of the local residents for military support or law enforcement purposes. There is also a Russian mafia presence in the region that conducts a lot of illegal activity like you described. The language they were speaking is a form of Turkic, not something Americans are used to hearing very often.

They found you because they had intelligence that you were in the area and were monitoring radio frequencies for activity. When the blizzard struck and you contacted the base using the shortwave radio, they picked up the signal and narrowed in on you."

Kate nodded, "How did *you* find me?"

"When you disappeared, we weren't immediately able to find and track the plane, but we did eventually figure out which plane you most likely left on. With that information we were able to determine the general direction it had traveled in and once we knew that, we just started rounding up the usual suspects in the area to shake them down for intelligence on your where-abouts. Based on what we already knew about the people who were looking for you, it was relatively easy to narrow down the search area.

Fortunately for us, the owners of the transfer point that was holding you decided they would rather make a significant amount of money by selling you to us rather than killing you as ordered. They had already been paid to kill you and Phillip had not required any proof. They double-dipped on you and did very well. Of course, they're in no danger of retribution because another team picked up Phillip and his crew while we were there."

"Isn't that negotiating with terrorists? I thought we didn't do that."

Brad laughed, "That's the dirty little secret, they're not terrorists. The reason the Chinese hadn't had any trouble in the region is because they are part of the peaceful Muslim resistance and they detest both the terrorists and the Russian occupation. So, while they appear to be working for the Russians, they're really working for the opposition and they help us with intelligence, for a fee of course. The money the owners of the transfer site and others raise from the U.S. and Russia goes to fund the opposition working within terrorist organizations to bring them down from inside. Unfortunately for you, other than the owners, the people who work at the transfer site think they are working for the Russians and to maintain their cover, the owners had to allow your mistreatment. Plus, they *really* don't trust Americans very much and think woman are second-class citizens. By the time we discovered you had moved through the site we knew the plan was to send you back if you didn't cooperate so we just sat around, monitored the area, and kept our fingers crossed that you would be disobedient so they would have to bring you back. The three days you sat in that cell so the owner's could collect their fee for 'killing' you from Phillip before we could get you out almost killed me." Brad hung his head, swallowed hard, and looked at the ground to compose himself.

"So if you knew about what Archie and Phillip were trying to do and what the program I was analyzing did, what do you know about the input program? You know, the program that was inputting information into the program Max had worked on that told the computer what bogus and disruptive orders to place."

"First, I need to say that we were still figuring out what the program that Max was forced to work on did at the same time you were, but we managed to decipher it about two weeks before you did. As far as the input program goes, you aren't going to like this.

Working together, the Russians and Chinese figured out how to imbed spyware deep inside computers' BIOS code. The BIOS code is the code invoked automatically as a computer boots up. The spyware was installed on computers manufactured in China and shipped to the U.S. and Europe, giving Russia and China access to a significant proportion of computers in those countries. Once the technology was out there, it didn't take long before it was in the hands of organized criminals within those countries. Until very recently, we didn't know it even existed, but we've executed bug fixes across every computer connected to the Internet within the past week, which should destroy their access.

One way they were using their access was to rapidly gather data from traders' computers about orders they were getting ready to execute. They ran them through an algorithm, then made disruptive trades based on that information. For example, if they knew a large number of sell orders for a particular stock were getting ready to happen, they would jump in front of them and sell a microsecond ahead of the orders and cause the price of the stock to plummet as the traders' orders came in. They would then buy the stock back when it hit bottom. Those were the mini crashes you were noticing and the reports you had from traders about stock prices moving before they hit enter on their orders. We knew the input program existed as part of another operation we were working on, but until you mentioned it, I hadn't connected it to Max's stock-trading program yet."

"How did you get the program Max worked on?"

"Max knew he would eventually be killed, so he printed the program and gave it to Phillip's servant to smuggle out of the compound. The servant managed to get it to some of the people we work with near the market who turned it over to us, for a fee of course. It was Max's last attempt to both stop the plot and get a message out to you."

Awareness of the danger she had been in suddenly crept into Kate's consciousness, "I'm glad you found me."

"I'm glad you remembered my grandmother used to call me Skeeter. You and my sister may be the only two people who know that and I was willing to extract whichever one of you was in that burka. I figured the odds were pretty good that it was you though." They smiled at each other.

"At some point during my imprisonment it became apparent to me that I was not running a safe house. The safe house was for me, wasn't it? Why didn't you just tell me?"

Brad looked at his hands again, " I was unable to convince the FBI that you were in danger, so I made you a contractor so I could get you into a safe house. If it makes you feel any better, you were running the safe house too and most of the people who passed through needed to be there. If I had told you that you needed protection, would you have believed me or allowed yourself to go to a safe house? I know you, you're stubborn, and you never would have gone." As Brad said it, a level of irritation arose in his voice as if he was preparing for an argument.

"You're right," Kate said calmly and Brad seemed to relax from his defensive position. "But why did these people want me?"

"When Max got to Singapore and started touring exchanges and trading firms, he started asking if anyone else had experienced orphan orders and discussed his suspicions about what was going on. This got the attention of one of their hosts, who was involved with Archie and Phillip. Max apparently also spoke highly of you, your skills, and how you had tried to help him figure out what the cause was. They knew Max was a potential threat to their operation, but they also believed you knew as much or more than Max did. To keep you safe Max allowed himself to be forced into helping them write their master program, but Phillip remained very concerned about you. They had started following you and even bugged your hotel room while you were in D.C. in an attempt to assess your knowledge.

This group was already on our radar and the intelligence community had been building a team for a while to increase our work on cyber-security issues in financial markets. That was one reason Harry Clark was sniffing around you, he wanted you on the team. Apparently, your being seen with me didn't help. Unaware of our previous relationship, Archie and Phillip's group assumed you were working with us, grabbed Max, and started watching you. I fear if you had left the country you would have been picked up even sooner than you were. Once we hid you away, that increased their interest in you and they became determined to track you down. I just knew I would never forgive myself if something happened to you," Brad frowned and squeezed Kate's hand.

"You said most of the people who passed through the safe house needed to be there, I assume Joe did not."

"No," Brad took a deep breath, "Joe is an Agency psychologist. I knew you were already somewhat depressed and frustrated with your work before Max died and with Max's death, being isolated in the safe house, and knowing what you were about to discover I wanted someone there to look after you. I wanted to make sure your emotional well-being was being cared for."

"So, if you just wanted me in the safe house, why give me the program Max had been forced to work on?"

"My reasons for that were twofold. First I wanted you to discover for yourself what had happened to Max, because I knew that was the only way you would accept it. Second, the program and the attempt to disrupt markets were directly related to your work and we wanted some help trying to figure out what was going on and I knew you wouldn't do it voluntarily. Now that you've done the work, you can also legitimately publish a paper about the causes of the mini-crashes. That discovery will both get you some acclaim and allow us to talk publicly about what we know, what we've done about it, and how to prevent future events."

Kate lay in bed frozen in a thousand yard stare directed toward the wall at the foot of her bed as another painful realization welled up inside her, "And you were my comfort guy. Your job was to make me feel good, to keep me motivated and on task." She adjusted her eyes toward Brad and focused an accusatory stare in his direction. Brad was looking at the floor and brought his hands up to cover his face.

With his face still covered, Brad whispered, "Yes, I…I suppose I was." He looked up at Kate with a pained expression and tears welling up in his eyes.

"Get out," Kate said harshly, wishing she were strong enough to yell. Brad didn't move. "I said, Get. Out." Brad stood and reached out to touch Kate's arm. She pulled it away. "Don't you dare touch me."

Brad walked toward the door. Once in the doorway he turned to Kate, "It's hard for me…I…I really do care about you very much." Kate said nothing and turned away allowing a single tear to run down her cheek as she felt herself harden and contract a bit inside. Now she knew why Brad couldn't trust anyone enough to have a relationship.

As Brad left, Kate noticed Joe standing just outside the door, he approached the bed, pulled over a chair and sat down. "Kate, I know you're hurting, but believe me, he loves you and wants to be with you. This is destroying him."

"Well, then. I guess Moriarty has left the building." Kate took Joe's hand in hers and squeezed it as she allowed herself to cry softly, about Brad and how she just became a little more like him. In the world that she and Brad now shared, people were either targets or assets and she realized she might never trust anyone again.

EPILOGUE

The July evening was cloudy and cool, so Kate lit a fire inside the screened porch in the fire pit Joe had made, her new golden retriever puppy resting comfortably at her feet. Having just finished an hour of target practice, Kate was cleaning her sniper rifle and sipping bourbon on the rocks.

It had been four months since her abduction and nearly two months since she had returned from the Mayo Clinic where she had undergone surgery to repair her shoulder. Physical therapy would be a big part of her life for at least the next six to eight months. Her paper on the causes of mini-crashes had been published a month earlier and her life had been a flurry of activity ever since with perpetual calls from reporters, congressional representatives, and lobbyists with requests for interviews, television appearances, and consulting. A cover story about how she had obtained the computer code and market data used in the development of her research had been created and Kate had told the story so many times the truth was fading into a haze. The portion of the truth Kate couldn't force out of her mind was her relationship with Brad. She hoped no one could see it in her eyes.

When she inquired, the CIA offered to sell her the cabin as government surplus for $100. Since its location was known, it was worthless to them as a safe house. The communication equipment was gone and the broken windows and much of the furniture had been replaced. While the blood and bodies had been removed, the pockmarks in the walls and ceilings from the bullets remained. The old communication room had been converted into a comfortable office. Kate used the cabin as a place to escape the ruckus her life had become. There were no phones or emails to answer at the cabin and for short periods of time Kate could reflect, write, and remember; she never wanted to forget what had shaped her into the person she had become.

Joe visited her at the Mayo Clinic and was the one who suggested Kate get a dog. He felt a dog might help her feel less lonely and learn to love and trust again. Kate had always enjoyed the companionship of a good dog and thought it was a good suggestion, but did not harbor the same hopes for herself that Joe did.

Joe was planning to visit Kate at the cabin in a couple of weeks, he too had some things he felt like he needed to work through in the solitude and history it offered. Unlike Kate, he wanted to put the incident behind him and felt staying there one more time and seeing the cabin again, as it had been when he first arrived rather than as it was when he left it, would be helpful to his closure. He told Kate he would never be able to give up her friendship, they had been through too much together and he didn't wish to suffer another loss. Kate's newly suspicious nature left her with a hunch that their ongoing relationship was less about true friendship and more about Joe being asked to continue to monitor her well being, but at least she did enjoy his company.

Kate planned to return to the university in August and continue to operate MAK Software on the side. The publication of her research paper had been good for MAK too, and they were opening a new branch to specialize in cyber-security. She had also learned that once you work for the CIA, intentionally or not, you never get to completely walk away. Kate was harder, stronger, and becoming more financially independent, but she preferred most the company of her sniper rifle and dog.